"Bree, open your eyes. Look at me."

Her eyes flew open. She gasped in surprise when Ryland swung out from the cliff, into the open air just past the truck door.

"Get ready," he told her. "I'm going to reach for you. You'll have to grab my hand."

He swung back toward the cliff. Hot tears coursed down her cheeks. Give up her hold on the truck and grab at him as he swung by? Impossible.

"Bree, I can't get any closer. Do you understand? On my next pass, grab my hand." He swung back toward the cliff. "Next swing," he called out. "That branch isn't going to hold. It's now or never. Reach for me, Bree."

His feet pushed off from the cliff again. He swung out toward her, closer, closer.

"Now, Bree. Grab my hand!"

She shoved with her feet, throwing herself out the opening toward him, a scream in her throat as she fell into open air.

SERIAL SLAYER COLD CASE

LENA DIAZ

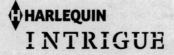

I couldn't live in my make-believe world, sharing my stories,
if it wasn't for the support of so many people, including
my family and these wonderful friends: Connie, Jan, Amy,
Alison, Angi, Jean, Donnell and so many more! I love you all.

HARLEQUIN®
INTRIGUE™

Recycling programs
for this product may
not exist in your area.

ISBN-13: 978-1-335-55565-6

Serial Slayer Cold Case

Copyright © 2022 by Lena Diaz

This edition published by arrangement with Harlequin Books S.A.

For questions and comments about the quality of this book,
please contact us at CustomerService@Harlequin.com.

Harlequin Enterprises ULC
22 Adelaide St. West, 41st Floor
Toronto, Ontario M5H 4E3, Canada
www.Harlequin.com

Printed in U.S.A.

Lena Diaz was born in Kentucky and has also lived in California, Louisiana and Florida, where she now resides with her husband and two children. Before becoming a romantic suspense author, she was a computer programmer. A Romance Writers of America Golden Heart® Award finalist, she has also won the prestigious Daphne du Maurier Award for Excellence in Mystery/Suspense. To get the latest news about Lena, please visit her website, lenadiaz.com.

Books by Lena Diaz

Harlequin Intrigue

A Tennessee Cold Case Story

Murder on Prescott Mountain
Serial Slayer Cold Case

The Justice Seekers

Cowboy Under Fire
Agent Under Siege
Killer Conspiracy
Deadly Double-Cross

The Mighty McKenzies

Smoky Mountains Ranger
Smokies Special Agent
Conflicting Evidence
Undercover Rebel

Tennessee SWAT

Mountain Witness
Secret Stalker
Stranded with the Detective
SWAT Standoff

Visit the Author Profile page at Harlequin.com.

CAST OF CHARACTERS

Ryland Beck—Lead investigator for the civilian cold case company Unfinished Business. He's also a former special agent criminal investigator with the Tennessee Bureau of Investigations. He lives in the Smoky Mountains near Gatlinburg.

Bree Clark—A detective with the Monroe County Sheriff's Office, two counties over from where Unfinished Business is headquartered. She's excited to assist Ryland on her county's serial killer case that went cold four years ago, a case she was unable to solve.

Dane Palmer—Head prosecutor for Monroe County. When a serial killer appears to resurface in his county following a four-year gap in killings, witnesses report seeing Palmer in the vicinity of each murder. He becomes the primary suspect.

Tommy Peterson—The sheriff of Monroe County micromanages what his detectives put in the official case record, which hampers the investigation. Does he not want the Slayer case to be solved?

Silas Gerloff—He's in prison for a road rage incident where he killed a driver who ran him off the road. Most recently, he was the cell mate of Liam Kline. He may have evidence crucial to solving the Smoky Mountains Slayer case.

Liam Kline—A businessman who was falsely convicted in Monroe County of possessing child pornography on his computer. Exonerated a few years later, he gleaned information in prison as Silas Gerloff's cell mate that might shed light on crimes committed by Dane Palmer and might prove whether the prosecutor is also a killer.

Chapter One

Maintaining a white-knuckled grip on the steering wheel while negotiating the treacherous curves up Prescott Mountain on his daily commute was typical for Ryland Beck. *Smiling* while he resolutely refused to look toward the steep drop on the other side of the road *wasn't* typical. Nothing, not even his phobia about heights, could dampen his enthusiasm this chilly October morning. Today he'd begin his investigation into a serial killer case that had gone cold over four years ago.

Bringing down the Smoky Mountain Slayer was the challenge of a lifetime. No suspects. No DNA. No viable behavioral profile. In spite of the lack of evidence, Ryland was determined to put the killer behind bars. He wanted to give the families of the five victims the answers and justice they deserved.

Unfortunately, what he couldn't give them was closure. Closure, as he well knew, was a fictional construct. The death of a loved one would always leave a gaping hole in the hearts and lives of those left behind. But knowing the victim's murderer had been caught and punished would go a long way toward making the excruciating grief more bearable.

He continued winding his way up the mountain toward UB headquarters as he considered the limited information he'd found on the internet about the killings. The Slayer's *modus operandi* was consistent: all of his victims were strangled, their bodies dumped in the woods in Monroe County. But aside from them being young women, the victimology was all over the place. Their educational and economic backgrounds varied, as did their ethnicity. Some were married, some weren't. Some had children, some didn't. All of that made it nearly impossible to build a useful profile to help figure out who'd murdered them.

The detectives from the Monroe County Sheriff's Office had deemed the case unsolvable. But here in Gatlinburg, Ryland had a unique advantage: an über-wealthy boss who knew firsthand the suffering a victim's family endured when a murder case went cold.

Seven years after his wife was killed and his infant daughter went missing, Grayson Prescott had given up on the stagnant police investigation. He decided to create a cold-case company called Unfinished Business. Just a few months later, UB had solved the case. Now, the thirty-three counties of the East Tennessee region had formed a partnership with UB and were clamoring for them to work their cold cases.

If those counties had the budgets they really needed in order to do their jobs, they wouldn't have to contract with a civilian agency to help them pro bono. Ryland had faced that same issue during his past career with the Tennessee Bureau of Investigation. How many killers had gone free because some bean counter valued money over lives? How many of those killers went on to murder other people? Those questions haunted Ryland. But his guilt was easier to endure knowing that the only reason he'd ever give up on a case at UB was if *he* decided it was unsolvable, not because of a lack of resources.

He rounded another sharp curve. A man was standing in the middle of the lane. Ryland slammed on his brakes, wrenching the steering wheel hard to the left. The man dove to the right, toward the drainage ditch. Ryland's Range Rover skidded sideways. His heart was in his throat as he wrestled with the wheel, trying to steer away from the treacherous cliff. The huge tires grabbed, held, then shot him across the road to the other side. He braked hard and came to a rocking stop inches from where the man had been standing just moments earlier.

A pent-up breath stuttered out of his lungs. Nausea roiled in his stomach. His hands ached from holding the steering wheel so tight. For several seconds, all he could do was sit in shock, thinking about what had happened, what had *almost* happened. He'd nearly catapulted off the mountain to certain death. And he'd almost killed a pedestrian too.

Meanwhile, the man responsible calmly stood up about twenty feet away, on the other side of the ditch that he'd apparently jumped. He brushed off his jeans, then smoothed his smudged white shirt into place, seemingly oblivious to his close brush with death. And in spite of the chilly temps, he wasn't wearing a jacket. What was he doing out here, on an isolated mountain, miles from town?

When he finally looked at Ryland, there was no fear in his expression, and no trace of guilt over standing in the road around a blind curve. Then he did the oddest thing.

He smiled.

It was a feral-looking smile, one that had Ryland instinctively tucking the edge of his suit jacket behind his holster, just in case the guy was about to draw on him.

As if reading Ryland's mind, the man's eyes narrowed. He snaked his right hand behind his back. And waited. Was there a gun in his waistband? A knife? Why was he acting so odd? Had he meant to cause an accident and was disappointed that he hadn't? If that was the case, he was dangerous, and needed to be stopped.

That thought had Ryland glancing in his rear view mirror, realizing that if another vehicle came around the curve and he was still sitting here, they'd have to swerve to avoid him. And if they didn't have a road-hugging four-wheel drive, they might not be as lucky as he'd been.

He jerked the Rover as far to the shoulder as he could and put on his hazard lights. He hopped out and was just starting around the hood when the man stepped into the woods and disappeared.

"Hey, mister, wait!" Ryland hesitated at the edge of the muddy ditch, hoping to catch a glimpse of the guy. But all he saw were bushes and trees.

"Mister, come back. I want to make sure you're okay," he called out. Under his breath, he added, "And that you don't play God with someone else's life out here."

Silence was his answer.

After a baleful look at the muddy water in the ditch, he backed up and took a running leap.

Chapter Two

Ryland shoved open one of the glass doors to Unfinished Business so hard it bounced against the doorstop and swung back at him. He managed to catch it just before it could slam into his face. He shook his head in disgust. A broken nose would have totally capped off this miserable morning.

His already painfully shrinking leather boots squeaked against the wood floor as he slogged to his desk in the cavernous two-story room to his left. All eyes turned to him, including Grayson and his wife, Willow, in one of the glass-walled conference rooms in the second-floor balcony at the far end.

Ignoring his audience, he yanked open his bottom drawer to get his go-bag of clothes and toiletries for unexpected last-minute flights or other emergencies. Today definitely qualified in the *other* category.

One of his fellow investigators, Adam Trent,

stopped beside his desk. His lips twitched as he struggled to suppress a grin, and whatever sarcastic comment he was contemplating.

A fat blob of mud chose that moment to slide out of Ryland's hair and drop on the folder in the middle of his desk.

Trent eyed the mud, then Ryland, his mouth curving with amusement. "Did you visit Old MacDonald's farm on the way to work?"

"Not another word," Ryland snapped.

An even larger blob of mud splatted onto the floor.

Trent howled with laughter.

Ryland aimed some colorful phrases his way and grabbed his go-bag. "When you manage to stop laughing, make yourself useful. Tell security to be on the alert for a possibly armed, middle-aged white male roaming the woods just down the road. I'll alert Gatlinburg PD after I change clothes."

Since Trent was still laughing, Ryland wasn't even sure he'd heard him. He gritted his teeth and trudged past the entrance toward the bathrooms on the right. Every squeak of his ruined shoes was punctuated by laughter coming from the room he'd just left.

"Um, excuse me," a feminine voice he didn't recognize called out from behind him, near the entrance. "Can someone help me find Ryland

Beck? I'm Detective Bree Clark with the Monroe County Sheriff's Office. I brought the boxes of files and evidence from the Slayer case."

"Yes, ma'am." Trent was still chuckling as he responded. "Hey, Ry, hold up. You've got a visitor."

Ryland whisked open the bathroom door and escaped inside.

RELIEVED TO HAVE finally finished transferring the physical evidence from the Slayer investigation into UB's evidence room, Bree Clark adjusted her skirt and sat in the guest chair beside Ryland Beck's desk.

Ryland, using the dolly Bree had brought in her police-issue SUV, deposited the last of the twelve boxes of case files on the other side of his desk, before taking his seat.

She was about to hand him the chain-of-custody forms, but hesitated when she noticed a mud-splattered folder in front of him.

He grimaced and tossed the folder into a drawer. "Is that the inventory list we were marking off earlier?"

"Yep." She set the papers in the spot he'd cleared. "Since you already initialed each item, all you have to do now is sign the first and last page, then verify the contact information.

When you're ready, I'll brief you and your team like we agreed—"

"Ryland." One of the men several few desks away was holding up a phone and motioning toward him. "Gatlinburg PD has more questions about that guy you saw."

Ryland gave her an apologetic look. "Sorry. There was…an incident on my way here and I need to take that call. Be right back."

She nodded, wondering if the incident he was referring to explained the mud and tears in his suit when she'd first seen him. When he'd returned wearing jeans and an emerald-green shirt that emphasized the green of his eyes the muscular contours of his chest, she'd forgotten all about the mud. Instead, she'd focused on trying to act professional and not let him see how rattled she was.

Even now, watching him across the room talking on the land-line, it was hard not to stare. But no matter how well he filled out those jeans, or how impressive his biceps were, what really mattered, what had to matter, was whether or not he was the top-notch investigator she'd been told he was.

When her boss had informed her that Monroe County would partner with UB to have their cold cases worked, she'd been more than a little worried. It didn't reassurc her that UB had been vetted by dozens of agencies, or that their investigators were all former law enforcement. Her concern was what they were now—civilians. Which meant they operated by their own rules, without the oversight she and her peers had. One wrong step, one illegal search, could lead to a judge throwing out critical evidence. A case could go from cold to un-prosecutable in an instant. It was her deepest fear that UB would accidentally destroy the chance of ever getting a conviction in the Smoky Mountain Slayer case.

Earlier, as she and Ryland had carefully checked off each piece of evidence and locked it up, there was no denying he *seemed* to know what he was doing. But it was still hard to take him seriously when he could have passed for a male cover model.

As if sensing her perusal, he glanced across the room and smiled. She smiled in return, then self-consciously turned her attention to the front wall of glass and the packed parking lot outside.

The dozen or so people in this massive squad room didn't account for the large number of vehicles. And since most of the walls were glass, she could see everything at a glance. Aside from the bathrooms and what appeared to be storage closets to the right of the main entrance, the building seemed to consist of this one large room and some stairs at the far end that led to a balcony of glass-walled conference rooms.

Maybe there was a basement and the drivers of the other vehicles worked there. One of the doors by the bathrooms could conceal another staircase instead of a closet. It certainly wouldn't be unusual in this area to have a basement. Most of the buildings were tucked into the sides of mountains, with a maze of support beams and stilts off the back, anchoring them into the bedrock. A lower level hidden from the front entrance would double the building's space. And it would provide spectacular views off the back.

"Sorry for the delay. You're probably in a hurry to brief my team and hit the road."

She turned in her chair just as Ryland sat at his desk, giving her another charming smile that had her pulse ratcheting up several notches. Good grief, he was sexy.

"No worries," she said. "I don't mind the wait." If it meant spending time with him, she'd be happy to stay all day.

"The Monroe County Sheriff's Office is in Madisonville, right? About an hour and a half from here?"

"Closer to two, especially if there's traffic. But I'm not in a hurry to head back. Don't get me wrong. I love my job and wouldn't want to work anywhere else. But I'm excited to meet more members of your team and get a feel for how you're going to approach the investigation. This is Monroe County's first time working with UB."

"It's nice to meet someone who loves their job as much as I do. Wouldn't trade mine for the world. As for this being the first case UB has worked for your county, that's true for most of the thirty-three counties we support. We've only been open for a handful of months. Initially, we worked from my boss's estate at the top of this mountain. This new building has only been open a few weeks and we're still settling in."

"I can understand that. My boss couldn't believe his luck when we came up in the queue so quickly."

"No luck involved. One of the perks around here is that each investigator takes turns picking a dream case to work. This was mine."

She stared at him in surprise. "Your dream case is the Slayer case?"

"Serial killer cold case. No DNA. No suspects. It'll be the most challenging investigation I've ever worked. What's not to love about that?"

She shook her head. "I hope you still feel that

way a few weeks from now. Once you get to the point of giving up, no hard feelings. If you manage to develop even one promising lead, it's more than we have now."

It was his turn to look surprised. "I have no intention of developing leads and moving on without fully exploring each one. If this thing *can* be solved, I'll solve it. I'm in this for the long haul."

"Good intentions are great and appreciated. But I'm not convinced you'll get any further than we did. We put a ton of work into the investigation and came up empty."

He leaned back in his chair. "I get the impression you're not a fan of involving UB."

Her face grew warm as she thought about just how vehemently she'd argued against hiring a group of civilians to work her team's case. But she didn't shy away from the truth. "Can't fault your impression."

He smiled at that. "What's your homicide clearance rate, Detective?"

"I wouldn't know. Calculating stats is my boss's job."

"Humor me. Take a guess."

She leaned back in her chair too. "All right. I'll play along. Seventy-five percent."

"Not even close. UB calculates the stats for each county we work with. Considering only arrest rates for murder, regardless of whether there was a conviction, Monroe barely tops fifty percent."

She winced. "How do we compare to our neighboring counties?"

"They range from fifty to sixty-one percent."

"Sixty-one? That's the best?"

He nodded. "Now consider just the cold cases. Investigations that are technically open, but unless a new lead comes in, no one's actively working them. There are several hundred thousand in this country. Of those, how many do you think are ever solved?"

"No idea. Twenty-five percent?"

"Try one percent."

She stared at him, stunned. "That's awful."

"Agreed." He motioned around the room. "The team you see here is dedicated to changing that statistic, at least for East Tennessee."

She frowned. "Doesn't seem like a big enough team to have a goal that lofty."

"It's small by design, at least for now, while we're still new and learning how to work together to our best advantage. Aside from our boss—Grayson Prescott—his wife, Willow, who's a part-time investigator and part-time victim's advocate, there's a special agent on loan from the TBI who brainstorms with us and provides law enforcement oversight like when we need a warrant, and eight full-time investigators."

"Eight? How do you expect to solve more than a few cases a year with only eight investigators? My team has five and we couldn't solve the Slayer case after a full year of working on it."

"Keeping the core team small helps us work better as a cohesive unit. Each of us has our own cases, but we meet regularly to brainstorm on all of the open investigations. If we need additional expertise, we bring on temporary consultants. In spite of operating for only a few months, we've started investigating twelve cold cases and have already closed nine."

"Closed, as in solved?"

"As in presented our findings and enough evidence, in our opinion, to prosecute each case. Yes."

"Wow. That's, what, seventy-five percent? A far cry from the one percent you quoted earlier."

"Full disclosure," he said, "some of the cases were chosen specifically because they appeared to be easy solves, not that any of them are really easy. But there was evidence that, if tested or re-tested with today's better technology, we strongly felt could lead to usable DNA profiles and potential hits on the FBI's DNA database,

CODIS. We needed those quick solves to garner confidence from the various law enforcement agencies we were trying to win over. It worked. Now they're clamoring for us to work their more difficult cold cases."

"Makes sense. I'm assuming you use all the latest forensic techniques, like culling public ancestry databases for DNA hits to come up with suspects?"

He nodded again. "Forensic genealogy is a favorite tool of ours. It was key to solving the first case we took on. Still a doubting Thomas about our abilities?"

She gave him a rueful smile. "I'm not quite ready to dust off my pom poms and cheer for UB. But at least now I understand why my boss was so excited about you working the Slayer case."

His eyes took on a teasing light. "Somehow I can't picture you as a former cheerleader."

She arched a brow. "I'm not sure whether to be grateful or offended."

He grinned. "Don't be offended. You've definitely got the looks for it." His face lightly colored. "My apologies. That was inappropriate."

She rolled her eyes. "I'm not someone offended by a compliment. That's what it was, right? A compliment?"

"Definitely."

"Then thank you. And you're right. I was never a cheerleader. I was one of the jerks making fun of the cheerleaders back in high school. Turns out they were smarter than me. A lot of them went to college on full cheer-scholarships. I had to flip burgers the whole way through."

"Guess we both learned the hard way. I stocked grocery store shelves during my college weekends and pulled occasional night shifts disinfecting a lab. But we'll keep that particular skill just between the two of us. I don't want the lab rats downstairs drafting me to help with cleanup any time soon."

"Downstairs? You have a lab onsite?"

"We sure do. The main lab's a few hours away. My employer funded an entire wing dedicated to processing our evidence before anyone else's. Here at UB headquarters, we have a much smaller annex. But, depending on the sample and types of tests appropriate for a piece of evidence, we can get DNA results back in days, or even hours, instead of months or longer in a typical overworked, underfunded state lab."

She groaned with envy. "Not fair. Are you hiring?"

He chuckled. "If or when we hire more investigators, I'll be happy to add your résumé to the hundreds we already have on file."

"Hundreds? Guess I'll keep my day job." She rested her forearms on the desk. "I'm truly impressed with what you're accomplishing here. And I'm actually starting to get excited to have you working on the Smoky Mountain Slayer case."

"Good to hear. I've been meaning to ask you why the killer is called the Smoky Mountain Slayer. I thought the Smokies didn't extend into Monroe County. But I'm a recent transplant from Nashville, so I don't know the eastern portion of the state all that well yet."

"I wouldn't know my way around Nashville either. But you're right. The Smokies aren't in my county. A reporter came up with the name and it stuck. I guess the Unicoi Mountain Slayer isn't as marketable as the Smoky Mountain Slayer." She shrugged. "Doesn't really matter. The Unicoi and the Smokies are both part of the same mountain chain, the Blue Ridge Mountains. And the first victim was found just inside our border with Blount County."

"And the Smokies *do* extend into Blount, I'm guessing?"

"They sure do."

"Whatever helps with news ratings, I suppose."

"I suppose. And believe me, the press in my county is notorious for gobbling up the smallest hint of a rumor and blowing it up all over the news feeds. They were broadcasting about the first murder before we'd even removed the body. AP picked it up, and it was sent all over the country."

He winced. "Makes it hard to keep details from the public during an investigation."

"No kidding." She motioned toward the dolly by the desk as she stood. "I'll return that to my SUV so I don't forget it later. I'm supposed to brief you and your team on the case, right? When is that scheduled?"

He grabbed the dolly's handle before she could. "I can get everyone together right after I put this in your vehicle."

"Did you forget I brought it in all by myself, along with the first load of boxes?"

"Only because I wasn't at my desk when you made that first trip. Please, I insist." He motioned for her to precede him to the door.

While she didn't need his assistance, it was nice being waited on for a change. The guys she worked with treated her as if she was one of them, which she appreciated most days. But being shown old-fashioned courtesy by a gorgeous and surprisingly smart man like Ryland was a true pleasure.

"Thanks. I appreciate it," she said. "And I just remembered there's a folder for you in the cab of my Explorer. It's got information you won't find in the official Slayer files."

Chapter Three

They both donned light jackets before heading outside in the chilly mountain air. Bree went to the cab of her white-and-green SUV while Ryland loaded the dolly into the back. She grabbed the folder she'd forgotten to bring inside and turned around just as he joined her.

He eyed the inch-thick, accordion-style folder with obvious reluctance as he took it from her. "I thought you had something *unofficial* to share. That looks like a pile of paperwork for me to sign."

"I wouldn't be that cruel," she teased. "This is a copy of my personal folder on the Slayer. My contact information on the inside flap. You're welcome to call me anytime, day or night, if you have questions. Or if you just want to update me on the status of the investigation. I'd really appreciate that, if you don't mind."

"Of course. I'd want the same thing."

She smiled her thanks. "The folder is chock

full of summaries and lists, lots of cross-refer-ences to the main files in the mountain of boxes by your desk. They should help you come up to speed fairly quickly. I included my personal notes too, for each of the five murders."

He leaned against the door, still not looking in the folder. "Personal notes?"

His wary look had her frowning in confu-sion. "Well, yeah. Didn't you include subjec-tive notes on cases, your impressions, things that didn't seem to add up, when you were a special agent? You worked for the state police, the TBI, before taking this job, right?"

"You did an internet search on me?"

"Of course. I wanted to make sure the lead investigator working my case was well-quali-fied before I turned everything over."

He arched a brow. "*Your* case? I thought De-tective Mills was the primary on the investiga-tion. That's what Sheriff Peterson told me when I requested the evidence and files."

Her cheeks heated. "Mills ran things, sure. But I helped. Our whole team did."

"And you've taken a personal interest in the investigation."

"Okay, I'm not sure where this is going. But, yes, this case matters a great deal to me. Five young women were senselessly murdered in my county by the same killer. I take that very personally. Wouldn't you?"

"Absolutely." His tone was even, matter-of-fact. "I just wondered whether you have a personal connection to one or more of the victims."

"If I did, I'd have taken myself off the investigation because of the conflict of interest."

"Good to know. And in answer to your earlier question, no, the TBI did *not* allow us to keep personal notes on the side. Everything, including my notes, was part of the official record. We couldn't risk a defense attorney accusing us of a Brady violation, withholding evidence. That could result in a mistrial, or worse, having the case overturned on appeal."

Her face heated again. Even though his tone was respectful, it stung having her methods questioned. She'd spent thousands of hours and months of her life trying to figure out who the Slayer was so she could bring him to justice. Being second-guessed by someone five minutes after handing over the investigation had her bristling like a porcupine.

"Thank you for the lesson on evidentiary procedures, *Detective Beck*. Apparently I was mistaken thinking you'd want a copy of my personal case file. You're welcome to cull through the dozen boxes of files inside UB and come to your own conclusions." She held out her hand for the folder.

"I didn't say that I wouldn't appreciate your notes, *Detective Clark*. I just wanted to understand why they weren't in the files you already gave me." He pulled the stack of papers from the accordion-style folder and started to skim them.

She crossed her arms. "Maybe if I worked for the TBI, or UB, I'd have the luxury of doing things the way you do. But Sheriff Peterson doesn't want feelings, impressions, or conjecture put into the record. And I don't want to lose that kind of information. My notes help me remember what I was thinking during an interview, the tone of voice used, their attitude, that sort of thing."

He glanced up at her. "You don't record the interviews?"

"Well, of course I do," she snapped, too annoyed now to soften her response. "But if I'm canvassing a neighborhood, going door to door asking questions, I don't have the luxury of a video recording. Later, at the office, I type up my notes for the case file, leaving out the subjective parts, *as required by my boss*."

He nodded, seemingly unfazed by the annoyance she'd been unable to hide as he slid the stack of papers back into the folder. He hesitated, then pulled out the thick envelope she'd included. "What's this?"

She let out an impatient breath. "Pictures. And before you ask, they're copies. The originals, at least the ones relevant to the case, are in the boxes I gave you. I wrote the name of each person on the back of each photo."

He slid the stack out of the envelope and tucked the folder under his arm so he could shuffle through the photos. "If some of these aren't relevant, why include them?"

"Oh, for goodness' sake. You're like a dog with a bone. At least I know you were serious when you said you wouldn't give up on the investigation. You never let anything drop, do you?"

His mouth twitched, as if he was trying not to smile, which aggravated her even more. She motioned toward the photos. "I was trying to give you context, to put faces with the names you'll read in the reports. I included everyone at the sheriff's office, even the admins in case you need additional copies of anything or have general questions about how we do things."

"Great idea. I wouldn't have thought of that."

"Will miracles never cease," she grumbled.

This time he did grin, but he didn't look up. Instead, he slowly fanned through the photos, showing far more interest in them than he had with her cross-references and summaries. As he flipped one over and read the name on the back, he frowned. "Why is a junior prosecutor in here? I thought this never went to trial."

"It didn't. But it was high profile, so we gave regular briefings to the prosecutor's office, at the request of the senior prosecutor. He wanted to continually evaluate whether we had enough evidence for a grand jury."

"And did you? Convene a grand jury?"

"No. We never got remotely close to having a viable suspect in any of the killings." She motioned toward his still-damp hair. "My turn. Since we're playing *Investigator Jeopardy*, I might as well ask the question that's been eating me up with curiosity since I walked into UB. You were covered in mud and your suit was torn. Mind telling me what happened? Was that the so-called incident you spoke to the police about earlier?"

He flipped to the next photo as he answered. "It is. I asked the police to patrol the mountain road, not that they agreed. They said they'd get to it when they can." He pulled another picture out of the stack and turned it over to read the back. "As to what specifically happened, there was a man standing in the road when I came around a curve on the way here. Luckily he jumped out of the way. Even luckier, for me, after swerving toward the cliff's edge to avoid him, I managed to *not* drive off the side of the mountain."

"Oh my gosh. How scary."

"Terrifying. He acted rather odd afterward. I'm convinced he wasn't in his right mind. No jacket, no backpack, no car parked anywhere to explain why he was there. And I'm half-convinced that he tried to force me off the road on purpose."

She stared at him in shock. "Did he admit that?"

"Before I could get close enough to talk to him, he took off. I'm worried he had a knife or a gun. That's why I asked Gatlinburg PD to come out here to look for him."

She glanced past the parking lot and road to the thick woods dotting the mountain side. "Was he right by UB when you saw him?"

"Close enough. About a half mile from here."

"And your torn, muddy suit? How did that happen?"

"When he ran into the woods, stupid me thought it made sense to go after him, so I hopped a ditch." He eyed her over the top of a picture. "My long jump skills haven't improved since high school."

She blinked. "You didn't make it across? You fell into the ditch?"

"Face-first."

She burst out laughing, then pressed her hand to her throat, heat rising in her cheeks again. "Sorry. I shouldn't have laughed. Couldn't help it."

"I don't mind you laughing. But if Trent does, again, I'll have to slug him. Or shoot him."

She chuckled, only half-convinced he was kidding. "Trent. He's one of the investigators I met while putting the evidence away, right? Someone you work with?"

"Unfortunately." His smile reassured her that he was teasing.

Some of the tension drained out of her. She hated that she'd been so aggravated with him earlier. Her temper rarely did her any favors. "What about the cuts in your suit? Did those happen when you fell?"

"My suit jacket caught on the bushes and tree branches when I tried to follow the mystery man into the woods. I only got a few feet in before I was forced to turn back. He seemed to know how to avoid getting skewered. I didn't."

The urge to laugh again was hard to resist. But she managed. Barely.

"The guy did me a favor in one respect," Ryland said, as he continued to examine the pictures. "Ruining my suit gave me an excuse to wear jeans. I hate suits."

Too bad. He looked great in them. Then again, he looked great in jeans too.

"Son of a... *That's him*." He held up one of the pictures. "This is the guy, the one who ran into the woods."

When she saw who he was talking about, she shook her head. "No way. That's Dane Palmer, lead prosecutor for Monroe County."

He frowned and studied the picture again. "I didn't get a good look at his face until after I'd almost mowed him down. By that time, he was standing on the other side of the ditch. But I'm telling you, this is the guy I saw."

"Can't be."

"Does Palmer have an identical twin? A triplet?"

"Not a twin, triplet, or quadruplet to be had. He's an only child. Ryland, I don't think you understand the significance of what you're saying. Palmer isn't some half-crazed criminal skulking around Sevier County running out in front of people's cars. He's probably the best prosecutor Monroe County—heck, Tennessee—has ever had. He wins almost every case he prosecutes. He's practically a legend."

She started naming off some of the more memorable cases. "He put away Silas Gerloff, that guy from the road rage incident a few years back. He purposely crashed his car into another guy's car because he got cut off. Then he gutted him with a knife." She shivered.

"And Dan Smith, the businessman who took a gun to work and shot his boss and three other people because he'd been fired. His lawyer tried to get him off on an insanity plea, but Palmer convinced the judge not to buy into that. Smith is in prison for life, no possibility of parole. There's the pedophile, Liam Kline. No, wait, his conviction was overturned. But that's a rarity for Palmer. Oh, and Nancy Compadre. You must have heard of her, even in Nashville. She's the young mother who drowned her two sons when she drove her car into the river, then claimed two Black men were responsible. And—"

He held up a hand to stop her. "Okay, okay, I get it. Palmer has done a lot of good for your county. But that doesn't change what I saw. Your prosecutor is the guy who almost sent me careening off a cliff this morning, then smiled like a psychopath and acted like he was about to pull a gun on me. I got a really bad vibe off him. I honestly feel he's dangerous, which is why I asked Gatlinburg PD to look for him. Maybe he's a Dr. Jekyll, Mr. Hyde kind of guy and all you've ever seen is what he wants you to see."

"You feel that strongly that he's the man you saw?"

"I'd swear it on a Bible."

She blinked. "A Bible? Really?"

"A *stack* of Bibles. King James version."

"Southern Baptist?"

"Born and raised."

"Wow. You really are serious. Give me a sec." She stepped away to make a call. A few minutes later, she returned. "You probably should have your vision checked since I'm *certain* you're wrong. But I can't *prove* you're wrong. Palmer took a vacation day today. He didn't tell anyone where he was going, which isn't necessarily a red flag. But I asked one of his guys to call his cell. Palmer didn't answer."

"Does he have a wife we can talk to?"

"Divorced. No kids. Lives alone." She yanked open the door and hopped into the driver's seat. "Get in. Show me where you saw this mystery man."

Chapter Four

Ryland held up a low-hanging branch so Bree's long blond hair wouldn't tangle in it. She passed beneath it, smiling her thanks as they followed the mystery man's trail. He felt that smile all the way to his gut. Bree Clark was incredibly appealing. And he couldn't really explain why.

She was pretty, certainly. And she had a knock-out figure that would make any man take notice. He'd practically drooled when he'd first met her and she stood to shake his hand, revealing sumptuous curves and gorgeous legs. But her appeal was so much more than that.

Maybe it was her fiery temperament, the confident, determined look in her hazel eyes, the impossible-to-hide honesty of her reactions. If she ever tried to make a living playing poker, she'd starve. Bluffing was a skill she didn't have.

It cracked him up how aggravated she'd been when he'd questioned her about her handling of the investigation. She'd obviously wanted to slug him. But she'd tried to pretend it didn't bother her, at least until she couldn't tamp down her anger anymore. It was refreshing to be able to trust someone's reactions. But her inability to conceal how she really felt was undoubtedly a challenge while interviewing suspects. He wondered whether her fellow detectives routinely made excuses to conduct interviews, rather than let her do it.

"Are you stuck in the bushes again, city slicker?" She glanced over her shoulder at him.

Realizing he'd slowed down while cataloging her finer points, he cleared his throat and jogged to catch up. "I'm doing just fine, forest girl."

She rolled her eyes and turned back, easily picking out a trail he'd never have seen on his own. And yet she followed it as if she'd been born with a special tracking gene. It was uncanny how she could spot a broken twig, a twisted blade of grass, a scuff in the dirt that could have been made by someone's shoe. Her ability to follow a trail was the only reason that Ryland hadn't insisted on leading the way. He'd much rather be the first one to encounter danger, but he'd lose the trail in about two seconds.

It shouldn't matter which of them went first. They both had law enforcement backgrounds and had their guns drawn in case the guy they were tracking really was dangerous and armed. But Ryland had been raised to be protective of women. It was practically killing him not to push her behind his back. Instead, he compromised by keeping watch on the bushes and trees they passed so he could jump in front of a bullet for her at the first hint of trouble.

Back in college, his friends had been well aware of his caveman protective streak and had teased him that he should go into the Secret Service. But since he wasn't willing to take a bullet for some *guy*, his potential career with the Secret Service had been doomed. Then again, if the president was a woman, maybe he'd sign up to be a human shield. He could think of worse ways to earn a paycheck.

They reached a clearing, and he finally was able to stand beside her instead of feeling like a heel following her. He was about to ask if she'd lost the trail when he noticed her face had turned ashen, her eyes haunted as she stared past his shoulder.

He whirled around, both hands tightened on his pistol as he swung it back and forth. But all he saw were the trees, deep in shadow since the thick canopy of branches overhead was blocking out the sun.

"Bree? What's wrong? Did you see him?"

"No. But I've seen *this* before." She motioned around the clearing.

He tried to see what she was talking about, but everything seemed…normal. Or, based on his limited experience, as normal as he thought a clearing *should* look in the middle of the woods. "You've seen *what* before?"

She jogged to a tree about ten feet away and patted the trunk. "North." She jogged to another tree. "East." Two more trees. "South, west. Do you see it?"

He was about to say no, but then he realized he did. "Four trees, forming a square if you draw a line around them. More or less."

"And each tree has some bark missing, a man-made mark showing it's part of the formation."

He looked again at the first tree she'd pointed to. Sure enough, there was a four-inch-long gash carved horizontally across the trunk about five feet off the ground, eye-level for someone Bree's height but a tad too low for him to have noticed at first glance. Each of the four trees she'd singled out bore a similar mark.

Tightly clutching his pistol, he scanned the forest around them again. "What do these marked trees have to do with the man we're looking for? Prosecutor Palmer?"

"He's not Palmer. You have to be mistaken."

He didn't bother arguing. She was still alarmingly pale. And since she refused to stand still, he was forced to follow her around the clearing, scanning the trees as he went.

"What are you doing now?" he asked.

She didn't answer. Instead, she paced off equal distances from each tree, finally stopping in the approximate center of the square they formed. Then she hiked up her skirt and dropped to her knees.

He swallowed, and tried not to stare at her glorious legs. Wasn't she cold? It had to be in the fifties up here. He was about to offer his jacket to put under her knees when she grabbed a stick and started digging.

He frowned. He didn't have a clue why she was digging. But he didn't like her being in such a vulnerable position when they still hadn't found the man they were searching for. He could be out here right now, hiding, watching, waiting for…something. Was he armed as Ryland believed? Dangerous? Maybe, maybe not. But Ryland couldn't shake the feeling that they weren't alone in these woods.

Leaving Bree digging, he walked the perimeter of the square, peering into the gloom, aiming his gun into nothingness. When he'd covered the entire area, twice, he relaxed, if only a little. In spite of his instincts screaming that someone else was out here, he hadn't found any evidence to back it up. There'd been no telltale flashes of jeans and a white shirt, no whisper of fabric as someone shifted position in some unseen hiding place. If there was someone watching, and he wanted to harm them, wouldn't he have done something already?

Heck, maybe the best strategy right now was to help Bree finish whatever she was doing so he could hurry her out of here, back to the office where she'd be safe. He grabbed another stick and dropped to his knees to help her dig.

He shoved the stick deep and scooped aside a layer of mud and leaves. A sickening stench filled the air, a smell Ryland had encountered far too many times in his career. Bree shot him a startled look and coughed into her hand.

Two minutes later, they found the first bone.

Chapter Five

Bree wrapped her arms around her waist and sent up a silent prayer for the victim and their family, while the Sevier County crime scene techs took pictures and placed evidence markers near the shallow grave that she and Ryland had discovered.

No matter how many murder scenes she'd been to, the senseless loss of life always hit her like a punch in the stomach. The usual heart-wrenching questions swirled through her mind. Did the victim know what was going to happen to them before it did? Was the end fast, merciful? Was it painful? Were they a husband, a wife, mother, father, sister, brother? How many others would suffer, their lives forever changed, because of this one person's tragic end?

She drew several deep breaths, fighting against the wave of anger and depression that threatened to drown her. This murder was hitting her even worse than usual, because it might have been committed by a killer she'd tried and failed to bring to justice. In a way, this person's death—whoever they were—could be, at least partly, her fault.

Get your emotions under control and act like a professional. You're not going to help the victim unless you pull yourself together.

Help the victim. Her internal voice was right. She needed to get a handle on her emotions. Only then could she work on figuring out what had happened, who'd done this, and stop them before they killed again.

Except that this wasn't her jurisdiction. And it wasn't her investigation. If this murder was linked to the Slayer case, UB would follow up with Gatlinburg PD, not her.

She fisted her hands at her sides, uncomfortable with her new role as a bystander instead of a participant. She watched the techs, the police milling around, the detectives pointing out things they wanted their techs to photograph and collect. Not offering her own suggestions, was one of the hardest things that she'd ever done. She wanted to explain to them, remind them, that one little fiber, one drop of sweat or saliva, could be the key to unraveling the Slayer's identity once and for all.

If this murder was the work of the Slayer.

Given what she knew about serial killers,

it didn't make sense that he'd go outside his geographical comfort zone when all the other killings had happened in Monroe County. But other things about him had never made sense either, like his inconsistent choice of a particular victim type, other than that they were young females.

This current scene also didn't fit with his modus operandi about what he did with the bodies. He'd left all of them in the woods. But until this one, he'd never buried any of them. Why change that now? Was it because this was the work of a copycat, and he didn't realize the previous five victims hadn't been buried?

The answer to whether or not they had a copycat was critical to both the Slayer investigation and this new one. If they were related, then all the information on the Slayer's prior crimes would be combined with this murder to try to create a workable profile. If they weren't related, evidence from the Slayer murders had to remain separate and not influence the decisions and conclusions made by the detectives.

A mistake in determining whether the killer was the Slayer or a copycat could be devastating, resulting in false leads, invalid conclusions, the wrong pool of potential suspects. A mistake like that could mean both killers remained free and neither paid for their crimes.

She desperately wanted to lift the tape and at least look at the grave. Maybe she'd notice something she hadn't earlier. No one had even touched it since she and Ryland had pulled out that bone. They were all waiting for the Sevier County medical examiner and his team to arrive.

The ME would preserve trace evidence on the body, giving them a better chance at solving the murder. But even knowing that, she still wished she and Ryland had dug a little more before stopping and calling the local police. They'd followed protocol, preserved the scene. Training and experience had overridden their desires to hunt for clues. But now they couldn't even be sure whether they were dealing with a male or female victim.

If they'd uncovered the skull, they might have found some hair to tell them length and color. The pelvis could help them guess whether the victim was male or female. Remnants of clothing might match pictures from missing persons cases and provide a tentative ID. Since they'd done none of that, now they'd have to wait days, maybe weeks, for the ME to share their conclusions.

She sighed in frustration and glanced to her right, where Ryland stood several yards away, talking with the owner of UB and several of

UB's investigators. It was only after they'd arrived that Bree had realized Ryland wasn't just one of them: he was their boss, UB's top investigator. He'd barked out orders, and the others had jumped to comply, securing the scene, stationing still more UB investigators at the road to direct Gatlinburg PD and the Sevier County Sheriff's deputies to the scene.

Her phone buzzed in her pocket. She pulled it out and checked the screen. Sheriff Peterson must have passed along the information she'd texted earlier about her and Ryland's discovery. This latest text was from Detective Mills, the lead over the Slayer investigation, back when there'd been an investigation.

How sure are you that the marks on the trees are the same as before? he texted.

As sure as I can be without a picture in front of me. Can you send one?

Hang on.

She would have sent him a picture to compare to the ones they had on file, but she knew better than to do that, and he knew better than to ask. Every picture taken of a crime scene had to be logged as part of the evidence. If someone saw her taking pictures, they'd confiscate her phone. Either with her permission, or courtesy of a warrant, they'd look through all of her pictures to make sure they retrieved the crime scene photos. They'd also look through her emails and texts to make sure she hadn't sent the pictures to anyone else. She'd be lucky if she got her phone back while it was still current technology.

The police weren't that strict in the past. But law enforcement had learned the hard way to be extra careful. As Ryland had reminded her earlier, anything a defense attorney could label as evidence could be used to work the system. A violent criminal could go free because of a legal loophole. She had absolutely no desire to be responsible for something like that.

Her phone buzzed again. She checked the screen and tapped the thumbnail image Mills had sent her. A close-up popped up of one of the trees she'd photographed, a picture that was already official evidence from one of the earlier Slayer crime scenes, so she wasn't violating any evidence protocols. She studied the image, then looked up at the nearest marked tree. Similar. But not a perfect match.

Then again, she didn't expect a *perfect* match.

Each gash was individually hacked and gouged into the trees. It would be impossible for them to be identical. But were they similar enough to conclude the same person had made both marks? She looked at the tree again, then the screen. Nothing jumped out as being all that different. But without being able to examine the tool marks, she couldn't be sure. Then again, maybe the Slayer had used different tools this time. He hadn't before. All the tool marks had identifiers that indicated they'd been made by the same tool—a hatchet, they believed.

Possible match, she texted back. Will try to get a close-up view again of one of the trees here to compare.

Three little dots popped up, indicating he was typing a reply.

Peterson just said not to spend more time on this. If copycat, not our jurisdiction. If it's the Slayer, UB can work on it. Brief UB, as originally planned, then come back.

She swore bitterly.

A few seconds later, as if he'd predicted her reaction, Mills texted one last word.

Sorry.

She couldn't help smiling. The two of them had worked together for years. He knew her well.

Not your fault. Will do. TTYL.

She shoved her phone in her pocket as Ryland walked up.

"Let me guess," he said. "Texts from the boss? Ordering you to back off?"

"One of my fellow minions, actually. But, yes, I've been reminded this isn't my case. I'm supposed to brief your team about the Slayer investigation, then head back to the office. Is the briefing still on? Given what's happened?"

"I'd still like to talk it out, if possible. But it might be a while. You and I will have to give written statements to the Gatlinburg detectives. And Grayson will want to compare notes with the rest of us. He's pretty ticked that someone else was murdered on his mountain."

She'd turned to watch the techs taking pictures, but Ryland's casual announcement had her whirling back to face him. "Someone else murdered on this mountain? This isn't the first body you've found here?"

He held up his hands in a placating gesture. "Take a breath and about three or four giant steps back from where that train of thought is taking you. The other Prescott Mountain murders have nothing to do with this."

She crossed her arms. "You haven't even read the Slayer files yet. You're not qualified to make the determination that these other victims you mentioned aren't his doing."

His jaw tightened. "Actually, I *am* qualified to make that determination. There was a serial killer operating up here in the past. That's one of the first cases that UB worked, and *solved*. There were no unanswered questions, no loose ends left to tie up. He had his own graveyard at the top of the mountain, in the woods outside of Grayson's personal estate. And his MO never wavered. The only thing in common with the Slayer is that both killers left victims' bodies in the woods, and they both buried them."

"I think you're making a judgment call you shouldn't, not until we get the evidence. But I'll drop it. For now. However, you're definitely wrong about one thing."

He arched a brow, his short-lived annoyance replaced with amusement. "What's that?"

"The Slayer didn't bury his victims."

He glanced at the shallow grave that was still waiting for the ME to arrive and finish uncovering its secrets. "Then either this isn't the work of the Slayer or he's changed his MO."

"Or neither of those alternatives."

He frowned. "You lost me."

"I've been thinking about how shallow the grave is. Maybe the body wasn't actually buried, not by human hands anyway. Falling leaves and other debris could have naturally covered it. Rain would make the remains sink into the ground."

"Fair enough. We'll have to wait for reports from the ME and the Gatlinburg detectives to see whether they agree with you. What's more important right now is figuring out the victim's identity, and how long they've been missing so a timeline can be established. Maybe things in Monroe County got too hot, forcing a switch in locations. Maybe your Slayer hasn't been dormant as long as you think."

She wrinkled her nose in distaste. "He's not *my* Slayer."

"Poor choice of words. Sorry about that."

She glanced around, then motioned toward the right side of the taped-off area. "Where'd your friends go? Back to UB?"

"Some did. The rest are hunting."

She blinked. "Hunting?"

"For the guy I almost ran over."

"I thought Gatlinburg PD was searching for him."

"They are. But my boss insists on helping with the search."

"Isn't he wealthy? Of the filthy rich variety?"

"If being a billionaire makes you filthy rich, then yes. Why?"

"I've never met a billionaire who risked his life searching the woods looking for killers."

"How many billionaires have you met?"

She chuckled. "You've got me there. But even not having met other billionaires, I'd be willing to bet your boss isn't like any of the others."

"Probably not. He's a brilliant businessman. But he's also a former army ranger. He's driven, tough, knows how to handle himself. And he's not the type to sit around and let others do the hard work when he knows he can contribute."

"Sounds like you really respect him."

"I do. He's a great guy, a really good friend."

"I'm surprised you're not helping him with the search."

He grinned. "You may have noticed that in addition to my poor long jump skills, I'm not exactly skilled in the tracking, hiking, or out-door survival arena. The Boy Scouts would have fled in terror if I'd ever asked to join them."

"No camping out in a tent for you?"

"My idea of roughing it is a hotel with less than three stars."

She rolled her eyes. "I don't believe that for a second. You like people to underestimate you, don't you?"

He didn't deny it. Instead, he motioned toward the grave. "Since you said the Slayer never buried his victims in the past, what made you start digging?"

"The marked trees."

"Given his history of not burying bodies, you didn't think maybe he'd marked the trees in preparation for leaving a body here?"

She flicked her hair back over her shoulder. "That's a logical conclusion. But I've been so convinced he stopped killing four years ago that I assumed this was an old body dump site we hadn't discovered. Based on that belief, I figured the body could have decayed into the forest floor, that we might have to dig a bit to find it. Of course, given the state of decomp, we know it hasn't been years. It's more likely a few months. But I didn't know that when I started digging."

"I don't think it's been months." He motioned toward the nearest tree wrapped with yellow tape. "That gouge in the tree's bark isn't weathered with age. It's the color of a fresh two-by-four from a box store. This is a recent kill."

Chapter Six

Bree shook her head. "I can't believe I missed that. Even with the awful smell when we opened the grave, I figured the body had been there a few months. Until the ME makes a determination, I guess we won't know for sure."

"What I want to know is how those over-zealous reporters you described in your county held back the information about the marks on the trees. Or did I just miss that while surfing the internet?"

"The press never knew about it. By the time I figured it out, the Slayer investigation was already going cold. The press had moved on to something else. Unfortunately, they're on the scent again. Someone stirred them up and they're hounding us, following detectives every time we head to a crime scene."

"What do you mean, someone stirred them up?"

She moved back so a pair of uniformed officers could get past, heading toward the road. "Shortly after UB notified us a month ago that this case was bubbling up in the queue, rumors started circulating around town. We've had citizens calling, asking if the killer is active again. We were all told to keep it under wraps that UB was going to get involved, but somehow it must have gotten out."

He winced. "That might be our fault. Our victim's advocate, Willow Prescott, spoke to each of the victims' families to make sure they were informed and had a contact to reach out to if they had questions. We didn't want them hearing it on TV first or through some other means. But even though we asked them to keep the information confidential, it's possible some of them told others and it spread around."

She sighed. "That's probably what happened. I didn't know anyone from your company was speaking to the families."

"Your boss did. We cleared it through him first. It's standard procedure for us to send a victim's advocate out before we start a case. Peterson provided us with the contact information for the families."

She clenched her fists beside her. "He should have told me, should have told all of us."

"How'd you figure it out? About the trees?"

"Changing the subject?"

His eyes sparkled with amusement. "Trying to."

She blew out a long breath and forced her hands to relax. "Okay, I'll drop it. But I'm definitely having a heart-to-heart with Peterson about the lack of communication when I get back. As to your question, I discovered the *murder-square*, as I call it, by accident. I was re-visiting one of the scenes and braced my hand against a pine tree to step over a dead branch. That's when I felt the cut in the bark. It was too straight and perfect not to have been done on purpose. Then I realized other trees had similar markings, and I compared them with photos from the earlier crime scenes."

His brows raised in surprise. "Your people took close-up photographs of all the trees in the general vicinity of where the bodies were found? At every scene?"

"No need to sound impressed. They weren't *that* thorough. None of the pictures from the other scenes showed cuts on the trees. I went back on my own, to each dump site. Sure enough, there were four scored trees at every location, forming a square with the body in the center."

"And a 911 call always initiated the discovery of each victim?"

"Yes. But it wasn't the killer making the

calls, if that's what you're thinking. We identified every 911 caller, ruled them out as suspects. Some of them discovered the bodies while hiking through the woods. One was camping nearby and heard some kind of noise, most likely an animal, and followed it to the scene. The last caller heard a dog barking and went looking for it."

His brow furrowed. "Did they find the dog?"

"No, and neither did we. The killer may have used a dog to lure the victim to him. Or just to ensure that someone discovered the body. Either way, that lead went nowhere."

They stood silently for several minutes, watching the organized-chaos around them. Crime scenes always reminded her of ants on an anthill. Watching everything as a whole made it seem pointless, like nothing was being accomplished. But watch one individual ant and it became apparent that he was accomplishing a specific goal, making progress that was otherwise hard to notice.

"Bree?"

"Hm?"

"If this recent murder was done by a copycat, they had to hear about the murder-square from someone. Who else knows about that?"

"My boss and the other detectives I work with. But if you're creating a suspect list in your mind, you can forget it. The guys I work with aren't murderers. What's more likely is that over the past four years, information about the crime scenes trickled out through innocent hallway conversations that were overheard. Or maybe loose lips at a party after a few drinks. It happens." She crossed her arms and leaned against the tree opposite him.

"It does. But let's assume that information didn't leak, that this latest killing is by the Slayer. That means the geographical area he prefers to kill in is much larger than once believed."

She briefly closed her eyes. "That idea has been eating me up since we found that bone. If true, it could mean there are more victims we haven't discovered."

"Maybe he only recently started up again, in this new location. He could have been incarcerated during the gap in the timeline and only recently got out."

"I prefer that scenario," she said. "Fewer victims that way. But I don't think it's likely."

"Why not?"

She turned to watch the crime scene techs as she answered. "His previous victims were always left where the likelihood of discovery was high. This place is remote, on a two-lane road up a mountain very few people have a legitimate reason to visit. It's not like Dollywood is at the top, or some other tourist attraction. The Appalachian Trail is miles away, so hikers aren't going to stumble across this place. And even if they did, without knowing about the murder square, they wouldn't know to scrape aside leaves and debris to look for a body. This screams copycat to me, a copycat who wasn't concerned about someone finding his kill."

"But he did want the body found."

She frowned and looked over at him. "What makes you say that?"

"Putting aside my belief that the guy we tracked to the grave is Palmer, and that Palmer is the killer, look at the logistics. The victim was left practically at the front door of the company where a group of investigators is about to begin work on the Slayer case. If the killer's from Madisonville, he probably heard the rumors, and that I'm the lead investigator. He deliberately targeted me, hoping I'd follow his trail, see the trees, and find the body."

"Even if that's true, all it does is confirm that the killer is likely from Madisonville. That doesn't exactly narrow the potential suspect pool."

"Then we start with the one suspect we do have—Palmer. We'll find out where he went today. And as soon as the victim's been identified, we'll work on a timeline of his, or her, last known movements, try to see if their path crossed Palmer's. We also have to dive into the original case files, review every Slayer murder from the beginning, look for new angles to explore." He gave her a sad smile. "Correction— *I* need to dive into the files. I keep forgetting you're not officially working on the case, that you have to go back to your job after we're done today."

She shook her head. "I wish I could stay and brainstorm with you. But I have orders, and a mortgage to pay, groceries to buy. Can't afford to just up and quit."

"Most of us can't." He gave her a sympathetic look. "I'll keep you updated. And when I interview your prosecutor as my number one person of interest, I'll keep you posted on his excuse for being up here, and whether he offers an explanation for how his trail could have led us to the kill site without him knowing about the body."

She chuckled. "You're not going to let that go, are you? You're positive we're after Palmer."

"I am until, or unless, I meet him in person, and he somehow convinces me that his doppelganger is running around Gatlinburg."

She laughed again, but her smile quickly faded. Everything they'd said was roiling through her mind. Several times she opened her mouth to speak, then thought better of it and kept quiet.

"You might as well say it." His deep voice was laced with amusement. "Whatever you're holding back is going to make you burst otherwise."

"That obvious, huh?"

"Completely. Go on," he said. "What else?"

"It's just that, well, when we made this discovery, I was convinced it was the Slayer's work. Everything points to it, so far anyway. If I assume he wasn't in prison and wasn't sick or anything, then I have to believe he just, what, decided to take a break? It doesn't happen. Serial killers escalate. They don't de-escalate. Maybe this really is a copycat. The what-ifs are driving me crazy."

His mouth quirked in a wry smile. "I'll play devil's advocate and argue with your scenarios. To start with, your premise that a serial murderer can't stop on their own is flawed because several have. I'm sure you've heard of Bind, Torture, Kill—the BTK Killer, in Kansas. After killing several people, he spent the next seven years focusing on playing husband and father before killing again."

"One exception doesn't destroy years of research into serial murder," she said. "Dennis

Rader, the BTK Killer, is an aberration, an outlier. As serial killers go, the example he presents is extremely rare."

"I'll give you another one, then. The Golden State Killer. Raped and murdered dozens, then abruptly disappeared from police radar. He was caught over thirty years later, but to everyone's knowledge, had never attacked anyone again during the interim. Wasn't incarcerated, sick, disabled in any way."

She shook her head. "You know your serial killers. I'll give you that. I'd argue that both Rader and DeAngelo, the killers you've referenced, would have continued killing if their obligations hadn't gotten in the way. They were both leading double lives, preoccupied with earning a living and supporting their families and pretending to be normal. No doubt they still had their sick urges, but didn't have the time or opportunity to act on them. Regardless, I'm not trying to win serial killer trivia. I'm just saying that if the Slayer was still free and able to kill, it's hard for me to imagine him stopping for four years. He was in an escalation phase back then, his kills getting closer together. I'm back to thinking it's a copycat. And before you warn me about jumping to conclusions, consider the guy who jumped in front of your car. We assume he's involved but he may not be."

He shoved his hands in his pockets and settled more comfortably against the tree. "How do you figure that? We followed his trail to the grave."

"His trail didn't stop at the grave. We stopped, because I saw the marked trees. Maybe he's not involved in any way." At his disbelieving look, she held up her hands in a placating gesture. "Just give me a minute here. I'm pointing out your investigative bias because you consider yourself an expert on Prescott Mountain."

"I *am* an expert on this mountain. I travel the road out front every day."

"But there's not a fence around it or a gate at the bottom to keep the riffraff out. The road up here is probably publicly maintained, right? Open to anyone?"

"It is. But—"

"But nothing. Have you noticed how incredible the views are up here? When there's a gap in the trees, at least?"

He gave her an odd look, but nodded. "Sure. The views are…great."

"I'm telling you, these are some of the best views for miles around. A moment ago, I said it was unlikely that many people come up this mountain. But I'm rethinking that. Some hiker or casual sightseer has to have stumbled onto this place and discovered its beauty. It only takes telling one other hiker to start spreading the word. It's one of the highest elevations in the area. And it's not saturated with tourists like Clingmans Dome, which makes it more appealing."

He gave her a grudging nod. "Valid points. It's a wider mountain than where the Dome sits too, with a more gradual ascent. Easier to hike, I suppose."

She smiled. "Exactly."

He crossed his legs at the ankles and glanced at the crime scene techs several yards away. "Do you always argue a point then contradict yourself with the next one?"

She laughed. "Probably. I sometimes drive my team crazy with my what-ifs."

"You're not driving me crazy. I find your mind to be quite…fascinating. Beautiful actually."

She blinked, her whole body going warm. "I, ah—"

"I'll allow that someone might come up here for the views alone," he said, steering them back to safer territory and helping to settle the butterflies that had taken flight in her stomach. "There's not much traffic here normally. And I assumed no one would come up here at all unless they worked for UB or were employed on Grayson's estate. But maybe some do. It's not like I watch the road all day to notice which people come and go. Heck, half the time I'm not at the office. I'm out interviewing potential witnesses or in other counties talking to detectives about their cold cases. Like this morning, I got here several hours later than usual for that very reason. I was wrapping up another case." He raked his hand through his hair, making it stick up in spikes.

She stepped closer and reached up and smoothed it down, without stopping to think about it. At his questioning look, her face heated. "I should have asked first. Your hair was sticking up."

"Thanks. I think." He winked, which had those dang butterflies taking flight again. "As to everything we just said, remember Occam's razor."

She nodded. "The simplest explanation is usually the right explanation."

"Exactly. I'm more inclined to think that if this is the Slayer's work, the most reasonable explanation is because he was incarcerated for the past four years. I can get a list of ex-cons who've been released into this area recently and cross-check that against any names that come up during the investigation."

"That'll be a long list."

He looked like he was about to reply, but they

both went silent as the medical examiner and his assistant finally arrived and picked their way toward the grave.

Their progress was slow. It was excruciating watching their painstaking work. But finally they pulled enough dirt back to fully reveal the skeleton—or what little Bree could see from her vantage point.

A commotion sounded from the other side of the clearing. Grayson, Trent, and two other men Bree had seen earlier at UB headquarters stepped out from the trees. When they spotted Ryland, they headed their way.

Trent gave Bree a polite nod, but addressed his comments to Ryland. "We followed the trail at least a hundred yards from here. But once we reached harder ground, we lost it. There weren't any more shoe impressions to find."

He was about to say something else, but stopped when two Gatlinburg police officers entered the clearing, escorting a man between them—in jeans, a white shirt and no jacket.

Bree blinked in shock. "Ryland, is that the man you saw earlier?"

His jaw was tight, his whole body tense. "No question." His gaze shifted to her. "Do *you* recognize him?"

Her whole body flushed hot and cold. "I want to say no. But I can't. That's Dane Palmer, senior prosecutor for Monroe County. And apparently, he's also the Smoky Mountain Slayer. I've been chasing the bastard for years and he was right under my nose the whole time. Those Gatlinburg cops have no idea who they're dealing with. They obviously haven't arrested him. He's not in handcuffs." She drew her pistol and started forward.

Chapter Seven

It had been a close thing when Ryland grabbed Bree's gun and tucked it out of sight before the police saw it. Would she have shot Palmer? Ryland didn't think so. But she'd been so angry that he wasn't sure. At the very least, she'd have been arrested for brandishing a weapon at a prosecutor, effectively ending her law enforcement career. Grayson and the UB investigators had formed a circle around her, blocking her from sight until Ryland could calm her down.

Once she *had* calmed down, she was horrified over her behavior. She must have thanked him and the others a dozen times. He'd then reminded her that they didn't have proof the prosecutor was a killer, in spite of how bad things looked right now. And it was because of that lack of proof that he hadn't been arrested. Then one of the crime scene techs had stepped forward with a wallet the ME found while moving some leaves from around the remains. The driver's license inside left no doubt as to the owner.

Dane Palmer.

When confronted by detectives, Palmer had emphatically insisted that someone must have stolen his wallet. The police had asked him to come to the station for questioning. He'd looked around like a drowning man searching for a life preserver. That's when he saw Bree and smiled. He'd immediately agreed to an interview, *if she was the one who conducted it.* Apparently he'd assumed she'd be a pushover, that she'd lob softballs at him.

He'd also insisted he'd only answer questions at a neutral location. He was worried about potential damage to his professional reputation if someone at Gatlinburg PD alerted the public and they saw him being brought into the station. That's when Grayson had stepped forward and offered UB headquarters for the so-called meeting.

As Ryland looked down the long conference room table where Bree sat across from Palmer, he was certain Palmer was regretting the agreement. Bree most definitely was *not* a pushover. A quick glance at Grayson and Trent beside him, then at the two Gatlinburg detectives at the far end, confirmed they'd all arrived at that same conclusion.

"Let's see if I have this right." Bree flipped through her notes on the legal pad in front of her. "You took the day off to run some errands in Madisonville, then headed to Gatlinburg."

"That's right."

"Because you wanted to check out the antique shops."

"I already told you this, Detective. My mother's birthday is coming up, and I always go antique shopping in Gatlinburg for the occasion. She collects Depression-era glassware. I was trying to find something she doesn't already have, in the patterns she likes."

"Really? My mom collects glass too. What patterns were you looking for?"

He crossed his arms. "American Sweetheart in pink and Paden City Ardith in yellow." From the smug look on his face, and the disappointed look on Bree's, Ryland guessed those must have been valid glass patterns.

"Very nice," she said. "But how did you plan on shopping for Depression glass without your wallet?"

His mouth compressed in a tight line. "I didn't *know* that I didn't have my wallet until I saw a technician holding it."

"You didn't notice it was missing when you tried to buy something?"

He yanked a set of keys out of his jeans

pocket and tossed them on top of the table. "See that miniature credit card on my keychain? I use that for most purchases. I didn't need my wallet."

"Easy enough to verify." She poised her pen to add more notes. "What's the name of one of the shops where you made a purchase?"

His gaze shot to the Gatlinburg detectives before he looked at Bree again. He cleared his throat. "I didn't buy anything."

She glanced up from the legal pad. "You didn't buy *anything*?"

His face reddened. "That's what I said, *Detective*."

"Why didn't you buy anything? You took the day off to shop."

"Obviously I didn't find what I was looking for."

"Right, okay." She set her pen down, a skeptical look on her face. "You don't have a receipt to prove you were downtown at the time when someone looking exactly like you, dressed like you, stood in the road and nearly caused Mr. Beck to drive off the side of the mountain?"

Ryland stared steadfastly forward, ignoring the look of concern Trent was giving him. It was damned inconvenient that Trent and all of his UB teammates had witnessed his height phobia first hand a few months earlier. With luck, that embarrassing episode would never happen again.

"Oh, for goodness' sake," Palmer said. "Jeans and a plain white shirt aren't exactly rare around here. And why would I stand in the road?"

"I can think of one compelling reason." Bree rested her forearms on the top of the table. "You wanted to toy with the UB team because you heard they were looking again at the Smoky Mountain Slayer cold case. You wanted to lead them to your latest kill and rub their noses in it."

His face turned so red that he looked in danger of stroking out. "You, Detective Clark, are way out of line."

"Just doing my job, sir. Asking questions that need to be asked."

He jabbed his finger in the air at her. "This isn't your jurisdiction. Don't tell me you're doing your job. Accusing a respected prosecutor of murder sure the hell isn't *doing your job.*"

She frowned. "Accusing you of murder? No, sir. Not at all. I was throwing out scenarios, hypotheticals in response to your question about why you'd be standing in the road."

He narrowed his eyes. "Are you trying to be funny? Because I'm definitely not laughing."

"Murder is never a laughing matter."

He swore and sat back. "My patience is wearing thin. We've gone over this already. I took a day off to shop, didn't find what I needed and was about to drive home when I heard on my scanner about police activity on Prescott Mountain. Out of curiosity, I drove up here to see what was going on."

"Do you realize how suspicious that sounds? That you just happened to show up at a murder scene where someone fitting your description is a potential suspect for the murder?"

"Ask anyone who knows me. I always listen to the scanner. If there's something major going on, I like to check it out. It's a way of keeping tabs on what's happening in the community."

"In your own county, maybe, sure," she allowed. "Why here in Gatlinburg? Wearing shoes that, by the way, appear to have a tread pattern consistent with the trail we were following."

He gritted his teeth. "They're a common type of walking shoe with a non-skid grip. Everyone around here wears them. As to the rest of what you said, my mother lives in Gatlinburg. It's my duty as her son to keep up with what's going on, to make sure she's in a good place, a safe place. I've always kept an eye on what the authorities are doing around here because of her."

"Right." She let the word hang in the air like

an accusation and took her time making some notes on her legal pad.

Ryland had to hold back a grin. She never raised her voice, never lost control. Instead, she was pushing Palmer's buttons, getting *him* to lose control. So much for being bad at interviews as he'd assumed earlier this morning. She was knocking this one out of the park.

She put her pencil down and calmly met Palmer's hostile gaze. "Where were we? Oh, yes. You drove up Prescott Mountain because you heard something going on over the scanner. Then what?"

He mumbled something under his breath that Ryland couldn't quite catch. He had a feeling that was a blessing.

"Sorry. What did you say?" Bree asked ever so politely.

He tugged at his shirt collar. "When I saw the police cars parked on the side of the road, I pulled over to ask what was going on. To my surprise, as soon as I got out of my car, two officers met me at my door. They said something about me looking like some guy the detectives wanted to talk to at a murder scene." He shook his head, clearly annoyed. "I graciously agreed to accompany them to answer any questions their detectives might have. Obviously if they wanted to talk to me about a murder around here, there was some kind of mistake. I was happy to clear it up. That's when that tech held up my stolen wallet." He looked toward the Gatlinburg detectives at the far end of the table. "Which, by the way, needs to be returned." He held out his hand.

One of the detectives shook his head. "Sorry, Mr. Palmer. The wallet was found inside a crime scene. It's evidence."

"That's ridiculous. At least give me my driver's license."

"You can apply for a replacement copy online."

Palmer glared at him and snatched up his keys. "If there's nothing else—"

"One more thing, if you don't mind." Without waiting for his response, Bree rushed to ask her next question. "How long has this day off of yours been planned?"

He frowned. "Like I said, I always take off right before my mom's birthday to shop for her gift. I do it every year."

"But when I called your office, they didn't know where you were."

He rolled his eyes. "A junior detective asks my assistant where I went on my vacation day, and you're surprised she didn't tell you?" He laughed. Bree's cheeks flushed a delicate shade of pink. "*Now* are you finished with your questions? Junior Detective Clark?"

"It's Detective, actually. No junior."

"If you say so."

A look of annoyance flashed across her face, but she quickly schooled her features. "I just want to remind you that you agreed to speak with me to allay suspicions, so the detectives from this county can move on to other potential suspects. Ending the interview now won't accomplish that goal. Perhaps you could supply us with a quick timeline of what you did today? That would go a long way toward alleviating any concerns."

The string of curses he let loose had even Ryland wincing.

Bree handled it with remarkable poise. When the prosecutor stopped swearing, she asked, "Is that a no? Sir?"

"You need me to repeat it to make it more clear?" Sarcasm dripped from every word.

"If you choose not to provide a timeline, it could prove…difficult…for the police to figure out when and how someone could have stolen your wallet and left it at a murder scene." She motioned toward the other end of the table. "I'm sure these fine detectives are willing to drive to Monroe County, if necessary, to partner with us in clearing up any remaining confusion. Sadly, their presence at your office will be noticed. And remarked upon. The sheriff, maybe even the mayor, might have to respond to questions from concerned citizens about why their esteemed senior prosecutor is being investigated in relation to a murder."

His eyes narrowed, but nothing could hide the look of malevolence in their dark depths. Had she pushed him too far? If he had nothing to do with this recent murder, or any of the others, then she was making a powerful enemy who could likely hurt her career. If he was the killer they were after, it could be dangerous for her to confront him like this, especially since they had nothing to hold him on.

Ryland glanced at Grayson, who appeared to be just as worried as he was. Letting Bree question Palmer might have been a mistake after all.

"Mr. Palmer?" She rattled the bear's cage again.

Ryland cleared his throat. "Perhaps we should end the—"

Palmer held up a hand to stop him, his gaze never leaving Bree. "A timeline? To help figure out who took my wallet?"

"Exactly. If, as you say, someone took it, then we need to find out who that was. You were the victim of a crime, after all. And it would help prove you weren't the person Mr. Beck saw earlier this morning." She tapped her pen on the legal pad. "What time did you last see your wallet, before the tech held it up, of course?"

He eyed her a long moment. Ryland was pretty sure *he'd* be squirming beneath that gaze, squirming to *punch* the guy. But Bree simply stared back, her expression serene. Either she didn't realize she'd stirred a hornet's nest, or she was much better at bluffing than he could have anticipated.

"Now *this* sounds like something worth exploring instead of your other questions that were a complete waste of my time." Palmer's expression turned less hostile. Perhaps he believed she was finally going to lob those softballs now. "I headed out the door at my house at precisely seven o'clock. My wallet was with me at that time."

She wrote the time and a note beside it. "You're sure?"

"Positive. I'm a man of routine, Detective. I make sure I have my wallet and my keys just before I leave the house. And since I planned on stopping at the dry cleaners down the street right after they opened, I'm certain of the time as well."

She wrote down the name of the dry cleaners that he gave her. "Did you go back home after that?"

"No. The clothes are hanging in the back of my car, clearly visible through the rear windows." He glanced toward the detectives. "I assume one of you noticed the clothes?"

They both nodded. Palmer smiled. "Now that we have that *very important* question settled, what's next, Detective Clark?"

"Walk me through where else you went, and provide the approximate times, please."

He rattled off the names, approximate addresses, and times for several other places where he'd stopped, including the library to drop off books and a box store to pick up some headphones he'd ordered.

"After topping off my tank, I headed up US 411 toward Gatlinburg, eventually turning onto 441. It's not a complicated route. I'm sure you traveled here the same way this morning. The only difference is the few twists and turns in Madisonville from my part of town to the highway, as compared to wherever you live."

"Which gas station, please?"

"This is ridiculous," he complained.

She simply sat, waiting, with pen in hand.

Ryland quickly did the math in his head, starting from when Palmer said he left his house. On a typical morning, Palmer couldn't have done all of that and made it up Prescott Mountain in time to be the guy standing in the road when Ryland was on his way to the office. But today wasn't typical. Ryland had run some errands of his own this morning for a case he'd just wrapped up. He'd gotten to work several hours later than usual. Palmer could still be the man who'd nearly forced Ryland off the road.

So what did that mean overall? If Palmer intentionally meant to be in the road when Ryland came up the mountain, had he done some surveillance of ahead of time? Did he know that Ryland would be running late this particular day? Or was this a reconnaissance run, he saw Ryland's Rover heading around the curve, and took advantage of the opportunity?

Palmer finally gave Bree the name and address of the gas station she'd asked about.

"How did you pay for your gas?" she asked.

He opened this mouth to respond, but hesitated, frowning. Then his expression cleared. "Cash. Usually I'd charge it, but I had some cash and wanted to get rid of it. So I went inside and paid."

"You wanted to get rid of it? Why?"

"Too much cash makes a wallet bulky. It's not comfortable to sit on, especially for a long drive. That's why I had my wallet in my console, because I… Hey, wait. I'll bet that's it. When I went inside the station to pay cash, someone must have taken my wallet out of my car."

Bree arched a brow. "At the gas station in Madisonville?"

"Yes. That has to be it. I don't remember seeing the wallet after that."

"You're saying that someone stole it, drove two hours away, and dumped it on Prescott Mountain at a murder scene, where you just happened to show up later to check on activity you heard over your police scanner?"

His face turned a mottled red again. "Thank you, Detective, for going through the logistics. Hearing it all together does sound farfetched. My wallet must have still been in the console on the drive to Gatlinburg. At some point *after* I got here, it was taken. Why, I don't know. Or for what purpose. Apparently whoever this man is that Mr. Beck saw and thought was me is the one who stole my wallet, then headed up this mountain. Heck, maybe he stole it because the two of us looked alike and he thought he could pass for me, use my credit cards. But he got spooked, dropped it, ran."

Ryland glanced at Trent, who shrugged. That was the first explanation Palmer had given that actually sounded feasible. Maybe the guy in the road really did have nothing to do with the murder. He ran from Ryland after the near accident because he had a stolen wallet. Was it possible he just happened to run near the gravesite and accidentally dropped the wallet? Had he stepped on it so it got shoved under some leaves? Maybe. But there was one rather large hole in that scenario.

Bree tapped her pen on the legal pad. "I'm still trying to understand how you and this mystery man, who could be your twin, ended up in the exact same location."

Bingo. That was the part bothering Ryland the most. Even allowing for the distance between him and the man by the road, he felt he'd gotten a good enough look at the guy to identify him in a line-up. And the guy he'd have picked in that line-up was Palmer. So the guy he'd seen had to be Palmer. Didn't he?

Bree gestured toward Ryland. "Mr. Beck is certain that you're the man he saw."

"Mr. Beck is mistaken."

"He's a former special agent with the TBI. He's trained to be observant, to notice the smallest details. He's prepared to swear under oath that you're the man he saw."

"Oh good grief. I'm an average-looking white guy wearing jeans and a white shirt. No tattoos, no distinguishing characteristics. Mine is not the kind of face that people tend to remember, Detective Clark. It's been the bane of my existence my whole life. In this instance, you're saying that because I'm an average Joe, and look like any other average Joe, I'm suddenly a killer? Give me a break. The whole idea is ludicrous."

Bree glanced at Ryland. The doubt he was starting to have was reflected in her eyes. She cleared her throat and gestured at the prosecutor. "Mr. Palmer—"

"No, stop. Not one more question. And just to be clear, I'll state this one more time. The first and only time I came up this mountain was when I drove up after hearing activity on my scanner. Since Gatlinburg PD was at my side from the moment I opened my car door, they can vouch for my whereabouts and the timeline of when I arrived. I would imagine that if they look through traffic video in downtown Gatlinburg, they'll see my car here and there to prove where I was and when." He motioned toward the media wall at the end of the room, dominated by a huge TV screen in the middle. "You'd think a company with access to the best equipment and technology money can buy would have better investigators. If they did, they'd know they're wasting your time, and mine, with this interview."

He shoved back from the table and stood. "This has gone way past the informal question and answer session that I agreed to. It's now harassment." He looked pointedly at the Gatlinburg detectives, then at Ryland and his team. "If anyone wants to talk to me again, they can submit a formal request to the prosecutor's office. And if you cause me any reputational damage, by the time I'm through, you'll all be lucky to have your jobs."

Bree's eyes widened, and she looked at Ryland again. He gave her a reassuring nod, but he didn't feel all that confident himself. Palmer wasn't like any prosecutor he'd ever dealt with. Ryland didn't doubt he meant every word of his threat to ruin their careers if they caused him trouble. While Ryland and his fellow UB investigators had nothing to worry about, Bree's situation was more precarious. She could lose her job over this.

Palmer motioned to Bree as if she was his assistant. "Drive me to my car. You can follow me back to Madisonville, and we'll head straight to the sheriff's office to see what he thinks of what you've done here today."

She made no move to stand. "My apologies, Mr. Palmer. I still have to provide a written statement about the discovery of the body in the woods. And then, per Sheriff Peterson's orders, I'm supposed to brief the UB investigators about the Slayer investigation. I'm sure one of the Gatlinburg detectives will be happy to take you to your vehicle."

He planted his palms on the table, leaning toward Bree. As one, Ryland, Trent, and Grayson moved to flank her.

"You need to leave," Ryland told him. "Now."

Palmer gave him a disgusted look and stalked out of the conference room.

Chapter Eight

Bree struggled to maintain her poise as Trent and the detectives followed Palmer out of the conference room. With most of the inside walls being glass, he could see her if he turned around and looked up at the second floor balcony. Not wanting to give him the satisfaction of knowing how badly he'd rattled her, she pretended indifference. But as soon as he'd been escorted out the building's main doors, she slumped in her chair and clasped her hands together, trying to stop them from shaking.

Grayson took the chair across from her that Palmer had vacated, while Ryland sat beside her. He shocked her by taking her hands in his.

"You okay?" Ryland asked.

She glanced at his large but surprisingly gentle hands covering hers, giving her the anchor she desperately needed. Her heart seemed to lurch in her chest, and she couldn't help wishing he'd hug her instead of just hold her hand.

"Bree?" His voice was as gentle as his touch, and filled with compassion and concern.

She cleared her throat. "I'm, ah, fine. Or I will be. Just need a minute." She couldn't quite manage a smile. "That was intense."

"You handled him like a champ. If you were nervous, it didn't show." He gently squeezed before letting go and sitting back.

The loss of his touch had her clutching her hands together again, to keep from reaching for him. Good grief. Why was she so needy right now? This investigation was really rattling her. Or was it just Ryland?

Since he was waiting for her answer, she tried to remember what he'd said. That she'd handled Palmer like a champ? That had her sitting a little straighter, some of her confidence finally, blessedly returning. "You really think so?"

"Scout's honor."

She blinked, then glanced across the table at his boss, who was watching both of them with open interest. She cleared her throat again. "You, Ryland, were never a Scout."

He grinned. "Guilty."

She laughed, which was a small miracle given what had just transpired.

"Better?" he asked.

And then she realized what he'd done. He'd

given her the strength she needed to move past her fears. Somehow he'd known exactly what to do, how to make her feel better. She unclenched her hands.

"I guess I am," she said. "Thanks to you. I'm feeling a lot better. In fact, I've gone from being totally freaked out to edging on furious. How dare a prosecutor treat me like that. *Junior* detective? *I'll regret this?* What the heck?"

"Is he always like that?" Grayson asked, reminding her again that it wasn't just her and Ryland in here, alone. And making her realize just how badly she'd like that—to be alone with him. Which didn't make sense, and was all kinds of wrong right now.

Focus, Bree. Focus on the case and answer the nice billionaire's question.

She arched a brow. "You mean is Palmer always a jerk?"

Grayson's mouth twitched, but he didn't quite smile. "I would have said something a bit more...colorful. But yes."

"Pretty much. But this, this was different. I've never seen him so..."

"Angry?" Ryland offered.

"No. Not angry. More like...out of control. Nothing rattles him, ever. To get so defensive, especially in front of anyone outside of the prosecutor's office, or even the sheriff's office, is completely out of character."

"This was personal," Ryland said. "He felt threatened and lashed out."

"Detective Clark," Grayson said. "How long have you been working with Palmer?"

She thought about the question. "I can't remember the first time I met him, but he was a Monroe County prosecutor long before I became a police officer. My best guess would be close to when the Slayer murders started, about five years ago. Five victims were killed in a twelve-month time span, and then nothing. Even though we never had a suspect, Palmer took a personal interest in the investigation and held regular status meetings with our department."

Grayson glanced at Ryland. "Is that unusual, in your experience?"

He nodded. "It happens, but it's rare. Bree, do you know why he was so interested in a case that didn't have any suspects? There was nothing for him to prosecute."

"He claimed he wanted to ensure we didn't make missteps that would jeopardize a conviction if it ever went to trial."

"Has he done that on other cases, before or after that one?"

She frowned, then slowly shook her head.

"Not that I know of, no. But if we assume he's innocent, not involved in the murders, I can sort of understand his motivation. He's a politician at heart. His reputation to the general public and media is everything to him. Given how high-profile the Slayer case was, he may have genuinely been worried we'd make him look bad."

Grayson nodded in agreement. "While *I'm* not an investigator, I deal with a lot of different personality types in the business world. Based on that, and from what I just saw, I think your assessment is spot-on. Palmer seems driven by ego, not a sense of justice. His lack of empathy was clear when he never asked about the victim, and didn't even bring up the possibility that the Slayer might be killing again. Although, to be fair, being questioned as a potential suspect caught him off guard, put him on the defensive." He shrugged. "We could be placing too much importance on the interview. Hard to say. Ry, what's your take? Could he be the Slayer?"

Ryland leaned back in his chair, facing Bree. "He lied about being on the road when I came around the curve."

"We don't know that he did," she countered.

"I saw him. I identified him in the picture you

showed me, then later in person when Gatlinburg PD escorted him to the crime scene."

"Eyewitnesses are notoriously unreliable, in spite of what I told Palmer. Even trained observers often disagree about *what* they saw, or *who* they saw, when giving accounts about the same incident. That's been scientifically proven in studies, over and over. It's why we work to gather hard factual evidence. And it's the main reason that groups like the Oversight Project exist, to review convictions to see if innocent people have been wrongly put in prison. People, eyewitnesses, make mistakes that put innocent people away. DNA and other scientific evidence have shown that time and time again."

"She's right," Grayson offered, as he pulled out his phone to check a text message. "When Willow and I were gathering information to start Unfinished Business, we reached out to the Oversight Project to get their take on the handling of cold cases. If I remember correctly, they told us something like seventy percent of the people they exonerated were convicted largely based on misidentification by eyewitnesses."

Ryland held up his hands in surrender. "Okay, okay. I'm willing to admit that it's *possible* the man I saw this morning wasn't Palmer. But he still stays on my persons of interest list."

Grayson put his phone away. "That was Chief Russo from Gatlinburg PD. As soon as Palmer's wallet was found, Russo's team started trying to trace his movements in Gatlinburg courtesy of traffic camera video. None of the cameras downtown picked up the prosecutor's car." He held up his hands when both Ryland and Bree started to say something at the same time. "Giving him the benefit of the doubt, he could have parked in a lot a few blocks back from River Road and walked. A lot of people do. It would explain his car not appearing on video. However, if he was truly shopping for dishes, those are heavy, and fragile, not something you'd want to cart around. I sure wouldn't."

Ryland nodded. "Which likely means he lied. The question is why. Is he trying to cover up involvement in the murder? Or something completely unrelated? Bree mentioned he's consumed with protecting his professional reputation."

"You're thinking an affair?" Bree asked. "Maybe with a married woman? I can see him lying to cover that up. Most people would."

"Absolutely," Ryland said. "Maybe he intended to shop for his mother's present later today and didn't want to admit where he'd really been. But if I was questioned about an alibi for murder, I'd give up names left and right to make sure the investigation didn't focus on me."

Grayson shook his head. "I've met a lot of narcissistic types, like Palmer appears to be. They're hard to predict, because they consider themselves smarter than everyone around them. He probably felt safe not revealing his secret since there isn't any hard evidence against him for murder."

Bree leaned against the table. "Sounds like you're both thinking he's *not* involved in whatever happened up on the mountain."

Ryland answered her. "That's for Gatlinburg PD to figure out. I need to focus on your cold case and let the police work the active case, at least until we find strong evidence to support a link."

"The marks on the trees aren't enough?" Bree asked.

"They're enough to support that a copycat could be active. Don't get me wrong, I'm not ignoring what happened today. But the cold case is my primary objective."

She sighed. "I get it. And as far as Palmer's concerned, in spite of how he acted in the meeting, I'm having a hard time seeing him as a violent offender. He may turn out to be, but in my experiences with him over the years, it doesn't feel right. Plus, there's another small thing that's been bothering me about him in relation to this case. It's, well, it's about the mud."

"Mud?" Ryland's brows shot up. "You mean, my muddy suit?"

"Kind of. You said the guy from the road jumped the ditch and took off into the woods. I know you were muddy earlier because you tried to hop the same ditch and missed."

He winced. "Thanks for the reminder."

She chuckled. "My point is that if the ground was so wet near there, with all that mud, how is it possible that Prosecutor Palmer's jeans looked clean, and there wasn't a hint of mud on his white shirt? Or even his shoes?"

Grayson sat back. "She's got you there, Ry. Didn't you tell me earlier the guy in the road had a smudged white shirt, as if he'd wiped dirty hands on it?"

He slowly nodded. "I sure did. I suppose Palmer could have a go-bag in his car, like we all carry. Heck, I've got one at home, my desk here, and my car. A lot of law enforcement does, in case they have to pull an all-nighter, or their clothes get messed up at a crime scene. Maybe Palmer realized he had mud on his shirt and exchanged it for a fresh one from his go-bag."

"Okay," Bree continued. "So then why cause

that near accident, run into the woods, go back to his car, wherever it was, and change his shirt, then come back about two hours later when all the cops were on the scene? It sort of paints him as an idiot, taking all those risks. And one thing for sure, Palmer is no idiot. He's cunning and smart."

Ryland tapped his hand on the table, a smile playing about his lips. "Maybe you should drop off your résumé after all, just in case a position opens up around here. Those are sound arguments."

A wave of pure pleasure had her stomach fluttering and her cheeks heating. If he'd told her she was beautiful, it wouldn't have made her go all mushy inside. But complimenting her brains had her wanting to melt into a puddle on the floor. "Thank you. So what do you say? Have we got one jeans-and-white-shirt guy or running around, or two?"

"I'm not ready to draw a conclusion," Ryland said. "But I'm leaning toward two. I'm also leaning toward my eyewitness account being far shakier than I'd thought. Hell, who knows? I certainly wouldn't swear it was Palmer I saw at this point."

Grayson stood. "If I'm not mistaken, that detective downstairs waving at us is the one who wanted you both to fill out written statements after interviewing Palmer. I suggest you do that as quickly as possible so we can move forward with the briefing about the Slayer case."

Bree and Ryland both turned to see the man he'd mentioned.

"I hate paperwork," she said.

"Necessary evil," Ryland teased as he too stood.

She started toward the door, then stopped when her phone buzzed in her pocket. She read the screen and groaned. "It's my boss. Palmer must have already bent his ear. I've been ordered to return to Madisonville, immediately."

Chapter Nine

"Stay here much longer and I'll charge you rent."

The sound of his boss's voice had Ryland looking up from his desk, surprised to see Grayson in the aisle with his arm around his wife's shoulders. Clearly he and Willow were on their way out. Ryland glanced around the squad room, stunned to realize everyone else had left and the fading sunlight was casting long shadows in the parking lot.

He pitched his pen on top of some folders and rubbed the back of his neck to ease the stiffness. "Can't remember the last time you two left before me. Heck, I don't even remember everyone else leaving. I must have zoned out."

Willow waved toward the stacks of files. "Fascinating reading?"

"More like tedious. These are the Smoky Mountain Slayer files. Bree warned me her boss is a stickler for keeping the records objective, facts only, no impressions or theories. She wasn't kidding. It makes for some dry reading. I'm not getting a feel at all for what the detectives thought about the various witnesses or even what direction they might have wanted to take the investigation if they hadn't been forced to move on to other cases. I need to meet with Bree and get her perspective. Unfortunately, she had to leave before providing that overview we wanted."

Willow smiled. "Are you sure that's the only reason you want to meet with Bree again? To get her perspective on the case?"

Grayson squeezed her shoulders. "Willow—"

She gave him an innocent look. "You did say they were holding hands in the conference room. Or did I hear that wrong?"

Ryland cleared his throat. "I, ah—"

"So you're heading to Madisonville to discuss the investigation, then," Grayson interrupted, giving Willow a frown that had her laughing. "How long will you be gone?"

"A couple of days, I imagine. I'll probably head there tonight so I can meet with her in the morning before she heads to work. It might be the only way she'll be able to carve out some time for me."

At Willow's wink, he rolled his eyes. As always, she was perceptive. There was no denying that his interest in Bree was more personal than it should be with him working a case for her department. But somehow he'd resist the temptation. He had to. He needed to focus and make sure the Slayer was brought to justice. And even if he didn't have the case to consider, the two of them lived a couple of hours from each other. That wasn't exactly a recipe for a successful relationship—especially since they both loved their jobs and neither was likely to consider quitting to move to the other's city.

And, good grief, he was taking leaps in thought that were ridiculous considering he'd only met her this morning. But it was hard not to take those leaps. It felt as if he'd known her for weeks, months, instead of only hours. The two of them just…clicked. Talking to her, brainstorming with her, felt so natural, so… right. And just thinking about her had his blood heating, his fingers itching to tangle in her hair and stroke her soft-looking skin. He'd have paid a small fortune to taste her lips, feel her curves pressed against him as he held her tight.

He cleared his throat, refusing to look at Willow for fear that he'd see his desires mirrored in her all-knowing eyes. Instead, he focused on Grayson to try to get the conversation—and his traitorous thoughts—back on track.

"Bree's boss had texted her to head back right after we spoke to Palmer," Ryland said. "But she stayed to provide that written statement Gatlinburg PD wanted. Unfortunately, her boss called again as she was heading out the door and was livid that she wasn't already on the road."

"Yikes," Willow said. "Sounds like a tough guy to work for."

He risked meeting her gaze again, but she seemed serious now, no longer teasing him about Bree. "I said the same thing. But Bree was quick to defend him, says he's fair and generous with praise and raises when they're earned. She claims he's just really particular and doesn't like surprises. She blamed herself, said she should have reminded him earlier that she was obligated to fill out the police report before leaving."

"Yeah, well," Willow said. "If my boss micromanaged me like that, I'd be out of there."

Grayson chuckled. "Since you have your boss wrapped around your little finger, I don't see that ever being a problem."

She grinned and stood on tiptoe to kiss him. It was probably supposed to be a quick kiss, but Grayson had other ideas.

Ryland cleared his throat, loudly. "If this is going to be X-rated, I need to head downstairs to the break room and get some popcorn for the show."

Willow laughed as she extricated herself from Grayson's arms. "Save the popcorn for another day. Come on, husband of mine. We have bags to pack, hotel reservations to make."

He kissed her forehead. "How about warm up the car? I'll be right out."

"I've heard that before. Ryland, don't you dare let him look at those files. He's a total wannabe investigator, and I'll never get him out of here if he starts reading the reports. Promise me you won't let him."

"Scout's honor," he told her.

She lightly punched his arm. "We all know that carries no weight with you. I mean it. Don't keep him long. We have plans. Oh, and when you see pretty Bree again, do hug her for me, won't you?"

Before he could think of a snappy comeback, she hurried out of the squad room.

When the front door closed behind her, Grayson perched on the corner of his desk. "Sorry about that. She's a matchmaker at heart. I shouldn't have let it slip about you, ah, comforting Bree earlier."

"Willow mentioned hotel reservations and bags to pack. Is there something you want to tell your second-in-command?"

Grayson smiled at his unsubtle changing of the subject, but didn't remark on it. "As a matter of fact, there is. I'm briefing the team tomorrow, but it looks like you'll be in Monroe County, so I'll tell you now. We've been corresponding with Katrina's *adoptive* parents ever since you located them." He shook his head. "I guess I should start calling my daughter Lizzie since that's the only name she knows. Regardless, a few hours ago, her…parents…agreed to meet with Willow and me. We'll be in Poplar Bluff, Missouri, for the next few days to talk through this mess and figure out the next steps."

Grayson shook his head. "When my first wife was murdered, and our baby girl went missing, I never could have predicted that almost eight years later I'd be planning civilized conversation with the couple who took Katrina and raised her."

Ryland stood and clasped his shoulder. "I can't imagine how hard this is. But I admire the hell out of you for how you're handling it. Most people wouldn't care that the Danvers didn't know Katrina was stolen. They'd take them to court and wrench Katrina—Lizzie—away from the only home she knows. Are you going to meet Lizzie on this trip?"

He let out a ragged breath. "Not yet. She'll

stay with a friend of the Danvers for the duration of our visit. We're feeling our way forward, figuring it out as we go. I want to be a part of my daughter's life, somehow. I don't want to traumatize her, though. It's not her fault what happened. But I'll be damned if she goes through life never being told who her real mother was. That wouldn't be fair to Maura."

"I'm sure you'll figure something out. You've got this."

Headlights flashed through the front glass walls. Grayson stood. "Looks like my time's up. Don't worry about anything here. I'll tell the team tomorrow about your trip to Monroe County. Trent can be my right arm while you and I are both away."

"Trent. Great. I'll have to clean up whatever mess he makes when I get back."

Grayson chuckled. "I'll be sure to let him know you said that."

"Please do. Go on, off with you before Willow comes in here packing a pistol."

"You too. Go home, Ry. There's nothing here that can't wait. See you in a few days." He strode across the room, and soon he and Willow were zipping out of the parking lot in his black Audi R8 Spyder.

Ryland grinned. He'd bought his Range Rover because it was like a mountain goat, with roll bars and a fancy, remote-controlled winch on the front in case he ever needed to pull himself out of an icy ditch once winter rolled around. Still, there was no denying the appeal of the sexy convertible Grayson drove. On a flat surface, it was probably a dream to drive.

After a frustrating search online to find a place to stay in Madisonville, he was forced to settle for an unappealing two-star motel in Sweetwater, about nine miles away. He sorted through the folders in the maze of open boxes beside his desk and pulled a few more out to add to the ones he'd already been reviewing. After topping off the stack with the folder Bree had made for him, he grabbed his go-bag of muddy clothes and headed out.

Rush hour was long over. Even stopping at his house first to pack a fresh duffel bag, he'd likely reach the hotel in less than two hours. It would be too late for a visit with Bree. But he could at least call her, see if he could bribe her with a free breakfast if she'd meet him before work in the morning.

It only took a few minutes to reach his cabin at the bottom of Prescott Mountain. He'd just finished packing and was heading through his kitchen toward the garage when his phone buzzed in his jacket pocket. As soon as he saw who was calling, he stopped and tossed the bag on the counter.

"Sheriff Peterson. How can I help you, sir?"

"Mr. Beck, Detective Clark didn't bother returning to work this afternoon, and she's avoiding my calls. I assume she's still with you at UB headquarters. Tell her if she doesn't call me in the next sixty seconds, she'll be suspended for a week without pay." The line clicked.

Ryland swore and immediately called the sheriff back.

Without preamble, Peterson said, "Bree? You using Mr. Beck's phone?"

"Sheriff, this is Ryland Beck. Bree isn't at UB. She left hours ago, right after filling out her written report for the police. Has anyone gone by her house to see if she's there?"

"What the… Are you sure? She left *hours* ago?"

He checked his watch. "It's seven o'clock now. Our interview with Palmer was over by two. It took both of us another hour, easy, to fill out reports and answer Gatlinburg PD's questions. By my calculations, she should have reached Madisonville a little after five."

"Well, I'll be damned. Hang on a minute."

Ryland leaned against the counter, tapping it impatiently as he waited. He didn't know Bree well enough to be sure how she'd react in various situations. But given her defense of her boss earlier, he was inclined to think she wasn't the type to ignore his calls.

He glanced at the digital clock on his stove. He'd been waiting for Peterson for at least five minutes. What was taking so long?

"Mr. Beck, you still there?"

"I am, yes, sir."

"I called Bree's neighbor, Mrs. Riley. She said Bree's police-issue Explorer isn't there, and her personal car's been in the driveway all day, as usual. Hasn't moved. Detective Mills contacted a friend at the phone company to ping her phone. They're double-checking, because they did this fast and might have made a mistake. But they gave me the GPS coordinates they triangulated based on the last time her phone pinged off any cell towers. I'm going to have my guys see if they can figure out the location."

Ryland was already bringing up a GPS app as he listened. "Can you give me the coordinates?"

"Texting them to you now."

Ryland checked his screen. "Got 'em. Hang on." He cut and pasted the data into the GPS app.

"I'll send someone by her house," the sheriff continued. "Just to make sure she's not there.

Maybe her SUV broke down and she accidentally left her phone in it after hiring someone to drive her home. That's the most likely scenario. I imagine she's still ticked at me. Maybe she decided not to bother coming in after all that." In spite of his words, there was concern in his voice, as if he was trying, hard, to convince himself something bad hadn't happened.

Ryland watched with growing trepidation as the GPS blip moved across the map, then stopped. He felt the blood draining from his face.

Bree had never made it off Prescott Mountain.

Chapter Ten

Bree's back ached from being jammed against the steering wheel. The pain was becoming so unbearable that she finally grasped the back of the driver's seat and pulled herself a few inches higher, shifting her position. The Explorer shuddered and rocked. She froze, not even breathing, until the movement stopped. Slowly, carefully, she let out a deep breath and reluctantly settled against the steering wheel again.

The irony of her current predicament wasn't lost on her. As a little girl, when she'd been in her dinosaur phase and begged her mom to let her watch a rerun of *Jurassic Park*, her mother said she was too young to see it. She'd worried that Bree would have nightmares about those "scary dinosaurs." Bree's dad didn't see it that way. And his soft heart couldn't deal with her tears when all her friends had seen the blockbuster movie and she hadn't.

He took her to the library on a Saturday morning, supposedly for some father-daughter time. After five minutes inside, so that he could honestly tell Bree's mom they'd gone, they took off down the street and watched a *Jurassic Park* classic-movie matinee at a dollar theatre. He'd been right about his tomboy daughter. She'd loved it. But her mother was right too. The nightmares were terrifying. She'd quietly suffered through them on her own, not wanting to get her daddy in trouble.

Now, here she was, a grown woman, living out one of the scenes from the movie. She was trapped in her crumpled SUV pointed nose-down toward the valley floor, suspended in the branches of some far too skinny-looking trees clinging to the side of Prescott Mountain. But unlike the little boy in the movie, she had no hope that Dr. Alan Grant was coming to her rescue.

No one was.

She'd accepted that depressing fact about two hours ago. That's when the battery had died, the post-crash alert system stopped flashing her emergency lights, and the horn stopped blaring.

With the pieces of her smashed cell phone sprinkled like glitter around the cab, the Explorer's 911–assist system was incapable of calling for help. And since her initial attempt to climb out the broken side window had sent the truck sliding down a good foot before jerking to a halt, she'd been trying *not* to move.

At some point, she'd have to accept that her only chance of survival was to leap out the window and pray she could grab a tree branch before the truck's downward plunge took her with it. But she hadn't quite figured out how to manage that.

She risked a quick glance over her shoulder where the windshield used to be. The view really was spectacular, with a full moon painting swaths of light across the valley floor. The trees were so far away that their autumn-dressed leaves sparkled like red and gold pixie-dust against a black velvet canvas. It was a lot like when her mom had taken her to the top of the Empire State Building. Except this time, she was about two Empire State Buildings up with no elevator to take her to safety.

The one blessing about her current situation was that if the seemingly inevitable happened, at least her parents wouldn't suffer, hearing how their only child perished. Bree had been their "surprise" baby late in life after they'd given up on being able to have children. Strangers had always assumed her mom and dad were her grandparents. It had bothered her, but they'd just smiled and never corrected anyone. They honestly didn't care. They were so grateful to finally have a baby that they didn't mind being the oldest parents at every birthday party or school event. Her mom had passed several years ago after a massive heart attack. Daddy died a few months later, supposedly of the same thing. But Bree had always felt he'd died of a broken heart.

She blinked away the tears tracking down her face, not daring to move her hand to wipe them away. And then she smiled, a bittersweet smile, as she thought about her one big regret—that she'd never get the chance to tell Ryland Beck she had a mad crush on him.

Was he attracted to her too? She thought he probably was, based on some heated, appreciative glances he'd thrown her way. And those sexy, charming smiles he'd gifted her with. Plus the incredibly sweet gentleness in his touch as he'd consoled her in the conference room. But she'd probably never know for sure.

In the short time since meeting him, she'd vacillated between wanting to drool all over him and wanting to yell at him. She couldn't remember the last man who'd gotten under her skin like that. It was maddening and exciting at the same time. Finding out whether the sparks between them would have led to fights or some really hot sex, and maybe something far more lasting and special, would have been fun. But even the possibility of exploring a potential relationship with him, after the Slayer case was over of course, had been eliminated in the span of a few seconds and one wild, terrifying ride over a cliff.

She shuddered, then bit her lip when even that slight movement had the truck bouncing in its precarious perch. When it didn't fall, she slowly inhaled, exhaled, no sudden movements.

And remembered.

She'd been driving down Prescott Mountain, rounded one of the crazy treacherous curves, then *bam*. A vehicle had slammed into the back of her Explorer. She'd been so busy fighting the skid, the last thing on her mind had been to glance in her mirrors and see who'd hit her. It had all happened so fast, a matter of seconds. It was impossible to regain control. And the guardrail, rather than stopping her two-and-a-half-ton truck, had acted like a ramp, sending her airborne.

As the truck somersaulted over the cliff, she'd screamed and twisted around, clinging to the seat back. For one millisecond, she'd glimpsed another vehicle up on the cliff's edge. It was a vehicle she recognized. After all, it had been in the city's parking lot every day since she'd joined the Monroe County Sheriff's office. The reserved spot had an elegant gold-and-black sign, declaring the name of the driver allowed to park there.

Prosecutor Dane Palmer.

Ryland had been right to suspect him of being up to no good.

A cool breeze blew through the holes where the windows used to be. Metal creaked and moaned. A loud crack sounded from the passenger side of the SUV. She looked on in horror as one of the branches snapped and fell away. The truck shuddered, then started turning and sliding sideways.

Bree grabbed the seat back and screamed.

Chapter Eleven

Ryland turned the Rover around at the top of Prescott Mountain, in front of the security gate that Grayson had installed several months earlier at his estate.

"Any luck?" Trent asked through the Bluetooth connection in the Rover.

"Zilch. I'm outside Grayson's place now. Didn't pass a single vehicle on my way up. All the guardrails are in place. Nothing broken that I could tell. Maybe the GPS coordinates Peterson gave me were wrong."

"Or maybe her phone battery went dead, or the phone quit working as she was heading down the mountain."

Ryland blew out a breath. "If that's the case, she could be anywhere between here and Madisonville, broken down, stranded. Do me a favor and call Peterson again, see if he can verify the cell tower information. And let me know what his people are doing on their end to find her."

"Will do. What about Gatlinburg PD? Did you call them already?"

Ryland made a disgusted sound. "They're the first ones I called. They gave me the standard answer police always give someone when they want to report an adult missing. Wait a few days and see if they show up. Without evidence of foul play or suspicious circumstances, they go with statistics, that the adult decided to take off on their own and will most likely show up again unharmed."

"Can't really fault them there. Most supposedly missing adults do show up, right as rain, nothing sinister to it. Maybe she was ticked at Peterson, like he said, and went somewhere to cool off before heading back."

"Come on, Trent. She's a police officer. She knows better than to worry someone like that. She'd have told Peterson where she is, even if she was too mad to head to the office."

"You're really worried about her, aren't you?"

He glanced past the guardrail, at the lights of Gatlinburg far, far below. His stomach knotted at the thought of her having gone over, plunging down into the valley.

"Ry?"

He shuddered and focused on the road. "Yes, I'm really worried about her."

"Well, she is kind of hot. She's got killer legs, a tiny waist, an impressive set of—"

"Grow up, Trent."

He chuckled. "Just keepin' it real, Mr. Doom and Gloom."

"Call Peterson back, all right? Get me new coordinates. I'll head down the mountain and take another look."

"Okay, okay. I trust your instincts. Something's really wrong." Worry and concern had replaced the humor in his voice. "Instead of calling Peterson, I'll get one of my contacts at the phone company to double-check everything. And I'll get some of the team on this to help with the search."

"Thanks, man. I appreciate it."

"Ry?"

"Yeah?"

"We'll find her. My ETA's fifteen minutes. Callum and Faith live fairly close. I'll get them out here quick, right behind me."

He tightened his grip on the steering wheel. "Let's hope I'm ruining everyone's evening for nothing. Thanks for having my back."

"Always. Talk to you soon."

Ryland headed down the mountain, creeping along with his headlights on their brightest setting, occasionally shining his flashlight out the side window. Whereas before he'd focused on the guardrails, this time he kept his gaze mostly on the asphalt, looking for skid marks.

The idea of anyone plummeting down the side of the mountain had his stomach knotting. But Bree wasn't just anyone. There was something captivating about her, something… special. The idea of something happening to her had his chest seizing up. She was so smart, sassy and full of life. And sexy as hell. His granddad would call her a spitfire, the ultimate compliment in his grandfather's opinion. She was definitely that, and more. Bree was a free spirit with a tenacious desire for justice, which was the ultimate compliment in *his* opinion.

God, please let her be okay.

He was halfway down the mountain when his phone rang. He pushed a button, answering through the truck's Bluetooth speakers again to leave his hands free.

"Ry, it's Trent. Those GPS coordinates haven't changed. But I did get more clarity around them. In this area, with spotty cell coverage, the coordinates are more of an approximation. Better than a guess, but way less accurate than they'd be in town."

"Well, that's something. Helps explain why I haven't found anything so far. How inaccurate are we talking? Miles off?"

"More like half the length of a football field, in any direction."

The hope that had flared inside Ryland disintegrated. "Then she still has to be on this mountain." He swallowed hard and glanced toward the nearest guardrail.

"I'll be there soon. I've got flashlights in my emergency kit. Faith does too. She's a couple of minutes behind me, Callum not much farther."

"Sounds good. When I finish this pass, I'll head up the most likely route she would have taken to Madisonville, just in case those coordinates are more off than your person at the phone company thinks they are. *Hold it.* I've got some skid marks here."

"Where? What's your location?"

He braked and leaned forward, peering through the windshield. "A little over halfway down. Give me a sec. I'm getting out for a better look." He shoved the truck into Park and hopped out with his flashlight, shining it on the dark marks on the pavement. Definitely fresh, and too far down to be the ones he'd made this morning.

Turning in a circle, he shined the light toward the ditch and the trees that went up that side of the mountain. Nothing. No trenched grass or broken limbs to indicate a vehicle had crashed through there. The shoulder on the opposite side was generously wide, with enough space for someone to pull over if they wanted to snap a picture or change a flat tire. Some of the skid marks led toward the guardrail, but it was intact, nothing to indicate a driver had lost control and gone over the side.

Something flashed in the light. He narrowed his eyes, carefully shining the light along the railing. One section, about ten feet long, reflected the light a little differently than the rest.

Because it was bent.

He ran toward the railing and stopped in front of the dented portion. Two of the posts in the middle had been snapped in half. But they were being held in place by the horizontal strip of metal. If he hadn't shined the flashlight just right, he'd never have even noticed it. All the other posts were intact.

His hand shook as he ran it across a streak of white on the metal above one of the broken posts. White flakes shot in the air like dandelion seeds. It was paint, white paint. The same color as Bree's police-issue SUV.

He aimed the flashlight over the railing, past the cliff toward the valley below. His knees nearly buckled when he realized what he was looking at.

About thirty feet down was the twisted wreckage of a green-and-white SUV with the words

Monroe County Sheriff on the tailgate and the driver's side. The truck was pointed hood down, but tilted toward the right. The only thing holding it up were the branches of some trees growing out from the side of the mountain under the cliff where he was standing.

His hands shook as he shined the light toward the driver's window, or where the window used to be. The truck suddenly shifted. Metal screeched. It slid down several inches before slamming against another tree branch and stopping again.

A scream filled the air.

His heart nearly leaped in his throat. "Bree?" he called out. "Bree? Are you in there?"

"Ryland! I'm here. Help me!"

The truck jerked again, sliding sideways a few more inches. *Crack*. A branch gave way, slamming against another one.

"Ryland!"

"Don't move, Bree!"

"It won't hold much longer. Please, help me!"

"Don't move," he repeated. "I'll be right back!"

"Don't leave me!"

The panic and fear in her voice cut him like a knife. But he couldn't waste another precious second if there was any chance of saving her.

He sprinted for his Rover and hopped behind the wheel.

"Ryland? What's going on?" Trent called out. "Did I hear someone screaming?"

"She's here, Bree. Call 911. Get the fire department up here. Somehow her truck flew *over* the guardrail and landed in some trees below the cliff. It's pointing nose-down and slightly sideways, barely holding. It'll go any minute." He slammed into Reverse and wheeled the Rover around to face the guardrail, then shot forward, skidding to a stop inches away.

"Are you kidding me? The car's in a freaking tree?"

"I'd try to attach my winch to the bumper of her SUV, but I don't think it would work. The truck's too heavy. It would pull mine down with it. Tell them to bring grappling hooks, a helicopter, hell, I don't know. Hurry!"

He grabbed the remote control for the winch and shoved it in his shirt pocket, buttoning it closed so it couldn't fall out as he ran to the front of the Rover.

"Ry, talk to me," Trent yelled through the Bluetooth speakers inside. "I'm calling 911 right now. Wait for the firefighters to get there. Don't do something stupid."

"I can't do nothing and let her die," he yelled back.

"If by doing *something*, it means climbing down a cliff without safety equipment, then you dang well better wait. Don't get yourself killed trying to do the impossible. It's too dangerous. Ry! Ry? Are you listening to me?"

"I'm a bit busy here. Did you call 911?"

Trent swore. "Wait right where you are. Calling them now." The line went silent.

Ryland pressed one of the buttons on the winch remote through his pocket. The engine whirred, feeding out steel cable. He pressed another button, stopping it, then grabbed the hook on the end. Now what? He needed some way to tie the cable around himself without it sliding up his body and him falling.

After a few agonizing seconds of pondering the problem, he threaded it tightly around and between his thighs, then attached the hook back around the main cable, forming a chair of sorts. He made it as tight as he could, hoping it couldn't slip off him even if he flipped over.

His stomach roiled. He squeezed his eyes shut, taking deep breaths, fighting back the darkness that threatened.

"Ry?" Trent's voice called out again. "Firefighters are on the way with a ladder truck. Wait by the road to flag them down."

He forced his eyes open and turned around to face the guardrail.

Big mistake.

The moon was bright tonight, bright enough to show him just how far down the drop was. Sweat ran down the side of his face in spite of the cold air. A buzzing noise sounded in his ears. Images flashed through his mind.

A cable car, high above the snowy mountains.

His father's face in the window, showing his disappointment that his spoiled teenaged son thought riding in a cable car was lame and had refused to get on.

Beside his father, his mom blowing him a kiss, forgiving him as she always did.

The cable car jerking, making an odd thumping sound, then climbing, sliding up the cable, higher and higher, farther and farther away.

A sickening screech of metal on metal. A pinging sound as the cable began to separate, flinging bits of metal out into the open air. Another jerk, the car swinging wildly. Screams of terror. A glimpse of his parents' ghost-white faces in that split second before the cable snapped and they plunged to the valley floor below.

"Ryland!" Trent and Bree both called out at the same time, snapping him back to awareness. He shook his head, desperately trying to clear the buzzing from his ears.

"ETA five minutes!" Trent's voice sounded from the speaker in the cab. "You there, buddy? Talk to me."

Bree didn't have five minutes.

He could do this. He *had* to do this. He drew several deep breaths, offered up a quick prayer and climbed over the guardrail.

Chapter Twelve

Bree clutched the driver's door, desperately trying to hold on as Ryland winched himself down the cliff face toward her. The truck's awkward downward and slightly sideways angle now was making it nearly impossible not to pitch out through the hole where the windshield had once been.

The truck wobbled and bounced, creaking and moaning as if in pain. The remaining branches wouldn't hold much longer.

She didn't know whether to thank God that Ryland was trying to save her, or curse him for risking his life. Could he even reach her once he was level with the truck anyway? The cliff face was at least ten feet away. If he thought he could climb onto the trees holding the truck, she'd have to warn him away. That kind of movement would send the truck crashing down, possibly pulling both of them to their deaths.

Creak. The truck jerked.

She let out a small cry, unable to stop herself. When Ryland didn't look down at her, she let out a ragged, relieved breath. His situation seemed almost as precarious as hers. She didn't want to distract him.

He was facing away from her, rappelling down in some kind of chair he'd fastened with the cable. His shoes scrabbled against the cliff face as he tried to keep himself from scraping against it.

Another creak. She squeezed her eyes shut. This was it. The truck was about to go. She didn't want to see the end coming.

Breathe in, breathe out. God, please let it not hurt. Make it quick.

"Bree, open your eyes. Look at me."

Her eyes flew open. She gasped in surprise when Ryland swung out from the cliff, into the open air just past the truck door.

"Get ready," he yelled. "I'm going to reach for you. I can only use one arm or I'll tip over. You'll have to grab my hand."

He swung back toward the cliff. Hot tears coursed down her cheeks. What was he saying? Give up her hold on the truck and grab at him as he swung by? Impossible.

He swung out toward her again.

"Bree, I can't get any closer. Do you understand? On my next pass, grab my hand and I'll pull you onto my lap." He swung back toward the cliff. "Next swing," he called out. "That last branch is bending and cracking. It's not going to hold. It's now or never. Reach for me, Bree."

He pushed off from the cliff again. He swung out toward her, closer, closer.

"Now, Bree. Grab my hand!"

She shoved with her feet, throwing herself out the opening toward him, a scream in her throat as she fell into open air, arms flailing. She missed! Impossibly, his arms wrapped around her, yanking her to him. The cable jerked. She was falling! She screamed. Another hard jerk knocked the breath out of her.

"I've got you. I've got you. Hold on. Grab hold, Bree. Wrap yourself around me. Do it!"

She was wrapped in an iron-tight bear hug against his chest. His legs were wrapped around hers. They were both hanging upside down, suspended from the cable.

"Grab me. Hurry! Before we hit the cliff!"

She squeaked in terror, wrapping her arms around his neck, holding him as tight as she could.

Crack! The shriek of metal filled the air. *Scrape, crack.*

"Hold on, hold on!"

She sobbed against his neck, digging into his

jacket, pulling his hair, whatever she could to keep from falling.

A tremendous rush of air shot out at them. Something sharp slashed across her arm. More cracks, popping noises, then…silence, for the space of a heartbeat. An incredibly loud bang sounded from far away. The world tilted crazily. The cable jerked and spun.

"Almost there, just a few more seconds."

Almost *where*?

"Hold on, Bree. Don't let go. I have to turn us or the guardrail will chew us up. Hang on."

The guardrail? She jerked her head around. They weren't upside down anymore. Somehow he'd flipped them over. She looked up just in time to see the flash of metal coming at them, fast. Or were they coming at the metal? She let out a small cry, certain it was about to slice into her arms around his neck.

His powerful thighs jerked beneath her. The cable whined and spun. His feet were braced against the side of the cliff just below the guardrail. His left arm remained tightly around her like a vise. He reached up and grabbed the railing with his right hand, jerking them against it. The winch stopped. Everything stopped. She stared at him in shock, his eyes inches from hers.

"Hard part's over, Bree. I need you to grab

the railing. These posts in this section are solid. Climb up and over. You can do it. I've got you. I promise I won't let you fall. Hurry."

There was something odd-sounding in his voice, something…off…that had her grabbing for the railing in spite of her terror that she'd fall if she did. She needn't have worried. He never let her go. He gripped the back of her skirt, steadying her, helping her until she scrambled over the top and fell down onto the other side.

Seconds later, he landed on the ground beside her, the cable whistling as it coiled on top of his chest. He lay there gasping for air, eyes closed.

Bree clutched his hand as they lay beside each other on their backs, a hysterical laugh bubbling up in her chest. It came out more like a whimper than a laugh, though.

His hand tightened around hers. "It's okay. You're okay."

"You saved my life, Ryland. I can't believe you did…whatever you did. But you saved me. Oh my God. What just happened? I can't believe any of that just happened."

She stared up at the canopy of trees overhead, trees that were safely anchored into the ground, not sticking out like bony fingers from the side of the mountain, cracking apart and slowly releasing their hold on her truck, on her. "I'm guessing that last bit of noise was my SUV plunging to the bottom of the mountain."

She drew another shaky breath. When he didn't say anything, she rolled her head to the side, looking at him. His eyes were closed, his face deathly pale.

She scrambled to her knees and leaned over him, searching for injuries. "Ryland? Ryland, are you hurt? Answer me."

"I'm. Okay." His voice was a thready whisper. Sweat poured off his face.

"Frankly, if he did what I think he did," a man's voice said as footsteps came toward them, "he's probably on his way to being catatonic."

"Shut up, Trent," Ryland whispered between clenched teeth, his eyes still closed.

Bree frowned in confusion as Adam Trent rounded the Rover and crouched beside his friend.

She looked down at Ryland. "I don't understand. What's wrong with him? I don't see any cuts anywhere."

"Just. Need. One. Damn. Minute," Ryland choked out, eyes squeezed tightly closed, his breaths growing ragged, strained.

Trent shook his head. "Ryland's got a bit of a fear of heights. We're talking full-blown clinical phobia, the kind where you get light-headed. Sometimes you throw up, sweat and eventually lose consciousness."

"Shut. Up." Ryland rasped, his voice barely audible now.

Bree stared at Trent, horrified. "Are you telling me he not only risked his life to save me, he lowered himself down a cliff knowing he could faint at any moment and fall to his own death?"

Ryland groaned.

"That about sums it up." Trent sounded ridiculously cheerful given the circumstances. "Wait for it. Wait for it. There he goes, folks."

Bree jerked back toward Ryland just as his arms fell to his sides and his jaw went slack.

Chapter Thirteen

Bree paced back and forth in Ryland's kitchen, talking to Peterson on the phone on what was turning out to be the longest day of her life. And it wasn't even eleven pm yet.

Ryland and his UB teammates waited in the family room. They'd all come to see him, to make sure he was okay after he'd refused to go to the hospital, like Bree. The only people who hadn't come over from UB were Grayson Prescott and his wife, Willow. Apparently some trip they were going to take tomorrow had been unexpectedly moved up, and they'd had to fly out tonight. But they were keeping tabs on what had happened and had been assured that Ryland was okay.

"Yes, sir," she said, in response to her boss's latest question. "I'm fine. I promise. Just like I told you the last six times you asked." She paused by the archway between the kitchen and family room, catching Ryland's questioning look from the couch. She gave him a helpless gesture and continued her pacing.

Peterson was still making sure she knew he wasn't pleased with her. "You should have gone to the hospital, Detective. At the very least, you need an MRI or whatever scan they do these days to check out head injuries."

"I didn't hit my head or ever lose consciousness. If I had, I assure you I would have gone to the hospital. But I didn't. Nothing's broken. Just a few bumps and bruises. It was the scariest experience of my life, but thanks to Ryland, at least I still *have* my life. Another few seconds and I'd have been compost at the bottom of the mountain." She shuddered. "Have you located Palmer yet?"

"We spoke on the phone. He's decided to stay in Gatlinburg to visit his mom for a few days before heading back."

"What? You didn't send someone up here to arrest him?" Ryland, Trent, and a few of the others looked at her through the archway. She mouthed a silent *sorry* for being so loud and paced the other way as she listened to her boss's lame explanation.

Stopping her nervous pacing, she leaned against the counter and stared out the back door. Ryland's yard was flat, with thick trees surrounding it, blocking any potential view of the mountains when the sun was up. Pretty unusual around here, where most people kept at least part of the brush and trees cleared so they could look out at the Smokies. But after learning about his phobia about heights, she could certainly understand why he didn't want the views. She was shocked he'd ever accepted a job where he'd have to drive up and down one of the highest mountains in Gatlinburg, given his fears. She was grateful he'd taken the job, though. Otherwise she wouldn't be here anymore.

When Peterson paused for a breath, she said, "Basically what you're telling me is that you don't believe me that he's the one who bumped into my SUV and sent me careening off a cliff. He's developing a pattern now. First Ryland, now me."

"We don't know that for sure."

"Don't we? The evidence is stacking up against him."

"You're jumping to conclusions. I can't speak to what Beck saw or didn't see. But what you saw was a car that looked like Palmer's. But you didn't actually see the driver. Unless you've thought about it and changed your mind?"

She clutched the edge of the counter in frustration. "No. I didn't see the driver. But what are the odds after everything else that happened today, with us knowing he was in the area, that someone driving a car exactly like his tried to kill me, without it being him?"

"Slow down, Detective. You're making assumptions without facts to back them up. I'll send Detective Mills up there in the morning to work with Gatlinburg PD to investigate the accident—"

"It wasn't an accident, sir. The guy pulled right up to the guardrail to gloat about what he'd done. If it was an accident, he'd have gotten out of the car and called down to me, asked if I was okay, called 911. Instead, he drove away. Like the coward he is."

"I'll agree they were a coward, whoever was in that car. But you don't know that it was Palmer. It could just have easily been some teenager who accidentally bumped your SUV. When he saw the aftermath, he was scared and took off. A hit and run. That kind of thing happens all the time."

"You're not even going to pursue Palmer, are you?"

He sighed heavily. "Yes. We're going to talk to Palmer, investigate what happened, see if he was involved. The truth will come out. And if I have to call the mayor to pressure Palmer to come in for an interview, I will. We'll get him on video and ask the hard questions. And I'll ask Gatlinburg PD to do a courtesy check on his car tomorrow, see if there's any damage."

"Tomorrow? Why not look at it tonight? You could ask Gatlinburg PD to go to Palmer's mom's house right now. We can't risk him fixing it if you wait. Or switching cars to conceal what happened."

"Are you listening to yourself right now? If he hit you as hard as you said, his bumper will be damaged. He can't fix and repaint something like that overnight. As for switching his car, come on, Bree. Gatlinburg PD will verify the VIN number against his insurance. This isn't their first gig. You're tired and not thinking straight. You've suffered a traumatic event. You're reacting like a victim instead of a detective."

"Yeah, well, there's a reason for that."

He chuckled. "I'll give you that one. Hang loose for a little while longer. You said you're at Beck's place right now. Where's it located? I can send one of our guys out there to bring you home. Obviously you won't be driving your police-issued SUV."

"No kidding." She speared a hand through her hair and shoved it out of her face. "His cabin's at the bottom of Prescott Mountain. But I don't see any point in making someone drive almost two hours to get me and two hours back.

It's already late. Ryland said I can use his guest room. And Faith, one of the UB investigators, was nice enough to pick me up a couple of outfits to choose from and some toiletries from an all-night box store over here. She even got me a phone since mine was destroyed. I'll be fine until Mills comes up tomorrow to investigate what happened. He can take me home when he heads back."

"That works. We'll talk again tomorrow. But don't plan on working for a while. I mean it. You don't come back to the office until you take a minimum of a week off. And when you come back, you'll have to meet with the department's shrink and get a note to return to active duty."

She clenched her hand into a fist. "I don't need to take a week off, or even a day. Physically, I'm fine. And I'm not suffering from PTSD. I have work to do."

"No, Detective. You don't. We'll divvy up your cases to the rest of the team, share the load. Can you imagine what a defense attorney could spin for a jury if he found out you worked on his client's case after a traumatic event, without taking some downtime and seeing a therapist? That reasonable doubt threshold would be gone. I'm not taking any chances. One week and a doctor's note. If the doc won't sign off after a week, you stay gone however long he thinks you need. I mean it."

"Sir—"

"No more arguing. That's an order. I don't want you calling for updates on the investigation either. As far as I'm concerned, you're a civilian right now. Rest, relax, no working on the case. And if something changes with your situation, if you even have a twinge of a headache or a weird pain somewhere, go to the hospital. Understood?"

Her shoulders slumped in defeat. "Understood."

"Good night, Detective."

"Night, sir."

"Oh, and Bree?" His voice softened. "I'm glad you're okay."

The emotion that leaked through his tone had her throat tightening. "Thank you, sir." She ended the call and shook her head.

"I take it that didn't go the way you'd hoped."

She turned to see Ryland, standing by the sink about five feet away. Her mouth went dry. Her arms ached to wrap around his waist, hold him tight. He'd saved her. Worse, he'd almost died doing it. What kind of man risked his life like that for a woman he'd only just met? She already knew the answer: a special, amazing man. A man she selfishly wanted to save her again, from the sea of emotions threatening to drown her.

He frowned with concern. "Bree?"

Reminding herself there was a roomful of people on the other side of the wall, she tamped down her emotions and put on a brave front. Or tried to.

"The call definitely didn't go the way I wanted. My *hope* was that my boss would take me seriously and go after Palmer. But he wants to take it slow and easy. Examine his car tomorrow, ask him to come in for an interview."

"What would you do in his situation?"

She was about to say she'd arrest Palmer, but instead of flippantly answering his question, she took a moment to think it through. She gave him a reluctant smile. "Honestly, without allowing emotion to cloud my judgment, I'd do the same thing as Peterson. Investigate. Gather the facts. Then decide on a course of action."

"Now there's the savvy investigator I met this morning. Although, after what we've been through together, it feels like we've known each other for years. Like we went through a war together and lived to tell the tale."

"Survivors," she whispered, barely able to force out the word. "We're survivors." The horror of everything that had happened slammed into her, leaving her shaking. To her shame, a tear rolled down her cheek. She wiped it away and drew several deep breaths, fighting to glue the pieces of her composure together before she completely lost it.

Suddenly his arms were around her, pulling her against his chest. "It's okay, Bree. Everything's going to be okay. You're safe. No one's going to hurt you here. Take it one step at a time. We've got this. Us survivors."

She threw her arms around his waist and melted against him, hugging him tight. If anyone else had offered her sympathy right now, and a safe place to land, she'd have broken, shattered into a thousand pieces beneath the weight of what had happened tonight. But somehow, Ryland's arms around her were the strength she'd needed to keep holding on. And she instinctively knew, no matter how hard things got, that he'd always be there for her. They'd formed an unbreakable bond tonight. And here, in his arms, she finally had what she'd been needing, the knowledge that she was safe.

A few moments later, the muted sound of someone laughing in the family room had her reluctantly pulling out of his arms and stepping back. She hastily wiped at the tears on her cheeks, her face heating.

"No rush," he told her. "We can stand here all night if that's what you need. Or I can hold you again, if that's what you want. Everyone else can wait."

She let out a shaky breath. "Careful what you offer. I was already crushing on you before all this, so it wouldn't take much to tempt me back in your arms."

A slow, sexy grin curved his mouth. "Consider me warned. Notice that I'm not running. I'm staying right here, with you. My offer's still open. And if you're not ready to talk about what happened, I can send everyone else home. They can come back tomorrow, or the day after that. Or never. You don't have to talk to anyone until or unless you're ready, and you want to."

She stared at him, slowly shaking her head. "You're an amazing man, Ryland."

His gaze locked on hers. His Adam's apple bobbed in his throat as he swallowed. Then he slowly closed the distance between them again. "Bree—"

She side-stepped him, her emotions too ragged to risk him touching her again, even though she wanted it, needed it, so badly she ached. Before, his touch had given her strength. Now she was afraid if he touched her, she would break.

He frowned and leaned back against the nearest counter.

She wrapped her arms around her waist.

"Your friends have been patiently waiting for me to get off the phone. They care about you and deserve to know the details about how you almost got killed."

His eyes widened. "This isn't about me."

"It's your team. Of course it's about you. I'm happy to tell them everything I can about tonight."

He frowned. "I don't think you understand why they're—"

"It's really okay. After we talk, I'll catch some shut-eye, then head to Madisonville tomorrow when one of my teammates picks me up. I'll be out of your hair, and you can get back to your usual routine." She headed toward the archway and into the family room.

Chapter Fourteen

Ryland recognized the signs of fatigue in Bree's posture as she curled her legs beneath her on the couch beside him. She was being incredibly patient, answering his team's questions, repeating the details as many times as needed. He filled in what he knew, trying to help. But she was the only one who'd been there when she was run off the road. And she'd been stranded for hours before he'd come along.

When Trent started to ask another question, Ryland held up his hands. "Enough. Let's stop the inquisition for the night. Bree needs to rest."

Her eyes widened. "No, no, it's okay. I don't mind answering more questions."

"I mind. You're exhausted. And to be honest, so am I."

"Whoa," Trent said. "You're not going to pass out again are you?"

Ryland narrowed his eyes. "Just remember, I'm the one divvying out assignments."

"Assignments?" Bree asked. "Are they helping you look into the Slayer case?"

"Sort of," Ryland said. "Chief Russo called me after you left UB earlier and updated me on the ME's findings. The murder victim we found has already been identified. Her name was Patricia Rogers. She was white, twenty-eight years old—"

"Wait," Bree said. "Patricia Rogers from Monroe County? *That* Patricia Rogers?"

"She's from your county, yes. I don't know if there's more than one person with that name there. Possible friend of yours?"

She scoffed. "Hardly. If she's who I think she is, I arrested her several years ago for attempted murder—of her five-year-old daughter. Palmer did everything he could to put her away, but the charges didn't stick. Not enough evidence to convince the jury. But she definitely did it. Thankfully, family services was able to terminate her parental rights and rehome her children with loving families."

"That's the basic background Chief Russo gave me, so I'm guessing the victim is the woman you arrested. I'm surprised your boss didn't mention it when he was talking to you earlier."

"I'm not. He's forced me to take a week off from work. He probably didn't want to tell me anything that might get me more interested in this recent murder investigation, emphasis on recent. I'm pretty sure I've seen Patricia around town at least a few times over the past month."

"That's spot-on with what the ME said. He figured one to two weeks. Gatlinburg PD is reaching out to an entomologist to try to narrow down the time of death estimate even further."

"Did he weigh in on whether he believed the body was intentionally buried, or it was concealed naturally, by falling leaves?" she asked.

"I haven't heard anything about that yet."

Trent cleared his throat. "Mind if I jump in here?"

"You already have," Ryland said drily.

Trent grinned. "Then I'll keep going. There are only so many coincidences that can happen before we agree they can't be coincidences. Palmer's name has come up too many times. The fact that he has a link to this latest victim seals the deal. He's involved in all of this, somehow. I'm inclined to side with Bree that he might be the one who forced her off the cliff."

She winced.

Ryland put his hand on hers. She gave him a grateful smile. But when Faith arched her brows from the other couch across from him, he cleared his throat and pulled his hand back. "Let's wrap this up. Bree, the main reason everyone is here tonight isn't to check on me. It's because when Grayson called earlier for a briefing on what happened, and I updated him on the ME's findings, he gave us a new directive. We're putting all of our other casework on hold so we can look into this latest murder, and what happened to you tonight, as well as the Slayer case to see how it relates to everything else going on."

Bree blinked in surprise. "Why would he do that? I thought you have to work cases for all the other counties."

"We do. Believe me, it's going to be a royal pain explaining to everyone that we're not actively working their investigations. But Grayson doesn't care. As he put it, he wants to make sure that no one else loses their life on his mountain ever again."

Ryland arched a brow at Trent. "That plays directly into your first assignment. You're in charge of guardrails. You get to head up a construction project to put a better safety barrier in place to help ensure another vehicle doesn't go off the side of Prescott Mountain."

Trent groaned. Everyone around him laughed.

Ryland continued divvying up assignments. "Lance, Faith, Asher, you'll shadow Gatlinburg PD on the investigation into Patricia Rogers's murder. Be sure to offer our lab's assistance. Nicely but strongly encourage them to allow an Amido Black test on the victim's skin for the killer's fingerprints. Obviously that's a long shot since the ME's report said very little skin remained on any of the remains. But if there are any testable areas, we want to do it. Make sure you let them know if they do end up getting fingerprints on the skin that way, there's a program the FBI has that can identify the victim's skin pattern and remove it from a picture, hopefully leaving just the killer's fingerprints. Our FBI contacts should allow them the use of that program.

"I'd also like you to try to figure out the identity of the man who was in the road this morning near where we found Rogers's grave. He looked like Palmer to me, which is really weird if he's not Palmer. Whoever he is, we need to know why he was standing in the road."

"You got it," Faith said.

"Trent, I'll give you a break even though you don't deserve it after teasing me. Have Brice help you with the guard rail project. You can both do some real investigating on the side. I want you to find out who clipped Bree's bumper. Make sure you personally see Palmer's car and can verify whether it's been in an accident."

"Trent," Bree said. "Palmer's still here, in

Gatlinburg. My boss should be able to provide his mother's address. Supposedly that's where he's staying, and where his car will be."

He nodded his appreciation, then gave Ryland a grateful look. "Thanks for letting me in on the investigation, in spite of the teasing."

"Don't be so quick to thank me. You and Brice have one of the hardest, most important jobs. We need to find out whether someone was specifically targeting Bree or not. If they're targeting her, we need to know why, and we need to know ASAP. If they tried killing her once, they'll try again."

Bree tensed beside him, her face going pale.

Ryland gave her a reassuring smile. "We're on it, Bree. Don't worry."

She nodded, but couldn't manage an answering smile. Ryland was getting more and more worried about her. He had a feeling she was near a breaking point.

"We really need to wrap this up," he said, noting how pale she looked. "The Slayer case, and any ties to the most recent crimes, becomes our main focus now. Ivy and Callum, starting tomorrow, you're going to live and breathe the Slayer cold case."

"And me," Bree said. "I can help too."

Ryland frowned. "You're supposed to be recuperating, not working. Your boss—"

"I'll deal with my boss. And I'm not about to sit around and do nothing while you're running the overall investigation. We both went through the same ordeal."

"Hardly. I didn't take a terrifying ride over a guardrail and hang in a tree for hours. My involvement was next to nothing compared to what you went through. You need to take it easy."

Her jaw tightened. "Not happening. If you don't want my help, I'll dig into this on my own. If it wasn't personal before, it is now. Don't try to shut me out."

"She has a point," Faith said. "I vote she gets to work on it."

"This isn't a democracy," Ryland said. "You don't get to vote."

Faith rolled her eyes.

Ryland shook his head. "Why do I get the impression none of you are nearly as intimidated by me as you should be?"

Faith grinned. "He caved, Bree. You're in."

Bree glanced back and forth between them. "He did? I am?"

Ryland sighed. "You are. For now. We'll see how it goes."

Faith gave Bree a thumbs-up.

Ryland couldn't help laughing. "All right. Everyone remember, even though we're splitting the team between two active case investigations and one cold one, we still follow standard procedures." He motioned to the dark-haired man sitting next to the very blonde Faith. "That means keeping our resident TBI liaison, Rowan, informed and involved in all decisions that can impact the future ability to prosecute any suspects we identify."

He checked his watch. "It's, good grief, almost two in the morning. Everyone get some sleep."

Everyone stood to go. Faith hesitated, glancing at Bree. "Are you sure you're okay staying here? I've got an extra room if you prefer to crash there."

Bree blinked. "I, ah—"

"She's staying here," Ryland announced. "Good night, everyone."

Faith's brows raised. She looked at Bree, waiting.

"I'll stay here," Bree told her. "But thanks for the offer."

"Anytime. Take care."

Soon, Ryland was locking the front door behind the last of the investigators. His shoulders slumped with exhaustion as he headed back into the family room. It was empty. Bree was gone.

"Bree?" He called her name and checked the kitchen first. Empty. "Bree?"

"In here."

He followed the sound of her voice down the back hallway to the guest room at the end. She was standing in the doorway, her face still alarmingly pale.

She gave him a tentative smile and motioned toward the bedroom. "I appreciate you letting me stay here tonight."

He hooked his thumbs in his belt loops. "You're welcome to stay here as long as you want."

Her eyes widened. "Did you forget my warning in the kitchen earlier?"

"If you're trying to scare me away, telling me you have a crush on me isn't the way to do it."

"That doesn't scare you, huh?"

He slowly shook his head. "Not even a little."

Her stomach jumped nervously. "Ryland, why do you have such a phobia about heights?"

He stiffened.

She stepped into the hallway and put her hand against his chest. "I'm sorry. I shouldn't have asked. Don't be angry."

He sighed heavily. "I'm not angry. Just... tired. Some other time, okay?"

He fingers flexed against his chest. "Of course. Ryland?"

His pulse thudded in his ears at the feel of her hand. "Hm?"

"I never got to thank you for saving my life. Do you mind if I thank you now?"

"You don't have to thank me, I—"

"I want to. Please."

"Ah, okay, sure. But I—"

She stood on tiptoe, then reached up and pulled his head down toward her. By the time he realized what he was going to do, she was plastered against him and kissing him the way he'd craved since the moment he'd seen her at UB headquarters.

She kissed him with wild abandon, stroking his tongue with hers, making him groan deep in his throat. He speared his hands through her long hair, turning and pressing her against the wall. Every nerve ending inside him was on fire, for her, as he took control of the kiss. It went on and on, until they finally broke apart, panting, gasping for breath, staring at each other in wonder.

Her passion-glazed eyes searched his, her lips slightly parted as she struggled to steady her breathing.

He was in even worse shape. There was no denying what that kiss had done to him. And when her gaze dipped down, her eyes widened, clearly seeing his predicament.

"Wow," she said. "Impressive."

He laughed. "Wow yourself. Feel free to thank me any time you want."

Her lips curved in a sultry smile. "I'm not warning you again. When this case, these cases, whatever—when it's over, maybe we can—"

"Oh. Yeah," he said. "Definitely."

She swallowed, then drew a ragged breath. "But right now, as much as I'd like to, we can't…you know…because, well, while we're working together in any capacity, even if I'm basically on leave, I should focus, you should focus. We can't…until…" She drew another ragged breath. "Good night, Ry."

He was careful to hide his disappointment as she turned back toward the bedroom. "Good night, Bree."

The door closed.

He stood there a long moment, still trying to get his breathing under control, not to mention the rest of his body.

Suddenly, climbing down a cliff didn't seem like such a big deal anymore. Not if it got that kind of reaction from Bree. He wondered if she'd still be interested in him if she realized just how hard he was falling for her. She'd no doubt been considering an affair, something short term. It would scare her right back to

Madisonville if she realized that he was already envisioning a possible future with her.

A future that would be dang near impossible since they lived two hours away from each other. Of course, that hurdle paled in comparison to the real problem.

Someone had tried to kill her today.

And they might try again.

He clenched his fists and headed down the hallway to his own bedroom. From here on out, he was sticking with Bree, whether she wanted him to or not. At least until they caught the guy who'd sent her over the cliff. Because even though it defied belief, she already mattered to him more than any other woman ever had. And he wasn't about to stand by and let some maniac hurt her.

Chapter Fifteen

Bree had originally refused when Ryland encouraged her to stay at his cabin while on leave from her job. But the appeal of him having her back if the man who'd forced her off the cliff came after her was too hard to resist. Especially since the identity of that man was still in question. According to Gatlinburg PD, Palmer hadn't gone to his mother's house as he'd told Sheriff Peterson he would. No one knew where he was right now. Which meant no one had seen his car, and whether or not it was damaged.

Bree, of course, believed Palmer had disappeared so he could get the damage fixed. All she could do was hope that once he finally reappeared, an expert would be able to determine whether the vehicle had been repaired. Of course, if it hadn't been repaired, then she was back to having no clue who was trying to kill her.

For the past few days, Bree and Ryland had spent their time mostly at his cabin, discussing the ongoing investigations and fielding calls from the UB investigators—with the exception of Ivy and Callum. Those two preferred to review the Slayer files on their own first, without being swayed by Bree's opinions or perspective.

Even though Bree longed to be officially back at work, it was no hardship waking up to gorgeous Ryland every day. Of course, waking up to him in the same bed as her would have been far better. But they were keeping things professional, or as professional as they could in spite of the undercurrents of attraction sparking between them. The memory of that earth-shattering kiss was never far from the surface. Pretending it had never happened was becoming more and more difficult. So when Ivy finally asked Bree to come to UB headquarters to give her perspective on the Slayer killings, she and Ryland had jumped at the chance.

Bree lined up five photos in the middle of the conference room table. "Now that I've provided the overview on the murder scenes and what we did to investigate the crimes, let's take it back to victimology. These are our five victims, during happier times obviously. Ada Cardenas was a single mom, never married, with one child.

Tammy Wilcox was also single, but no kids." She pointed to a third picture. "Robyn Morton, divorced, no kids. These two at the end are Candy Morrison and Joanna Sanford, the only victims who were married. Joanna had kids. Candy didn't."

Ryland looked across the table at Ivy and Callum. "The victims couldn't be more different physically either. As you can see, their hair varies from blond to dark brown, short to long, straight to curly. They're all relatively young, but there's still a variation in their ages. The main thing they seem to have in common is that they're attractive females."

Ivy idly tapped the table. "That's what Callum and I concluded too. What about geographical similarities? I don't know your county, Bree, so that's hard to glean just from their addresses."

Bree arranged the pictures into three groups. "These two lived in sparsely populated rural areas. This one lived in town just a mile from the Madisonville Sheriff's office. While she—" she pointed to the picture of Candy "—lived in the suburbs. And the very last one, Ada Cardenas, was actually the first victim. She's the one we found near the border with Blount County, in the foothills of the mountains. Of course, regardless of where they actually lived, their bodies were discovered outdoors, in wooded areas."

Callum shook his head. "Their educational backgrounds are different too. Four of the five were college-educated, middle class. But one never finished high school and lived in poverty, relying on social safety nets to help her make ends meet."

"Occupations are inconsistent too," Ivy said. "They were all paid by the hour as opposed to earning a salary. But some had blue-collar service jobs while others had white-collar office jobs." She sat back in her chair.

Bree crossed her arms on top of the table. "You're starting to run into the same roadblocks my team ran into. We couldn't find any ways where these five people's paths might have crossed. They didn't know each other. They didn't date the same people or have the same friends. They didn't even shop at the same grocery stores. While that makes it hard to figure out how they were targeted, it does reinforce the idea of a stranger as their killer. Our working theory was that these were randomly chosen victims of opportunity."

"No foreign DNA was found," Ryland said. "At any of the murder scenes, right?"

"Right."

Ivy blew out a breath, obviously frustrated.

"I don't like assuming these are all done by the same killer without forensic evidence to tie them together. But seeing the similarity in how the bodies were dumped, where they were dumped, and the fact that they were all strangled is certainly compelling."

"Did you notice the medical examiner reports?" Bree asked. "All of their fingernails were cut short, and bleach was used to wash their fingertips."

"Bleach." Ivy leaned forward, resting her arms on the table. "I totally missed that."

"Twelve boxes of reports are a lot to go through in just a few days." Bree smiled.

Ivy returned the smile. "Did he wash any other part of the bodies in bleach?"

"Just the fingers. Some of the victims had bruises on the sides of their rib cages. All of them had bruising on their necks. Our working theory was that he had each victim on their back and straddled them, his thighs pressed against the sides of their ribs as he strangled them. The bruising indicates he used his hands."

Callum straightened. "Were the necks swabbed for DNA?"

"They were. None was found."

Callum settled back in his seat, looking disappointed. "He wore gloves."

"Most likely. And his victims fought him, probably scratched him, which explains the clipped and bleached nails."

Callum slowly nodded. "Years ago, we would have profiled him as a cop or someone in law enforcement because he knows about forensics. He murders them somewhere else, then takes them to a dump site, minimizing the amount of forensic evidence we might find. Especially in the woods, where the elements and wildlife are likely to scatter and destroy anything of forensic value. And he uses bleach to destroy DNA."

"Years ago," Bree said. "But not now. Because everyone who has a TV knows about basic forensics."

He smiled. "Exactly. Really makes our jobs harder."

"It certainly does," she said. "There are more specific similarities in the autopsy reports, such as ligature marks and the types of bruises they exhibited. Again, working theory is that he abducts them, probably at gunpoint or knifepoint to get them to comply. Then he takes them to the primary site, which we believe might be his home, perhaps rural, isolated from anyone who might hear them scream. He ties them upright in a chair—based on the ligature marks—and, although he doesn't sexually abuse them, he does torture them. He has a fondness for knives, to cut, not to stab."

Bree looked at Ryland. "Has UB received a copy yet of the ME's report on Patricia Rogers? Did she have similar injuries?"

He shook his head. "Other than Chief Russo's phone call about the victim's identity, there hasn't been anything further yet from the medical examiner. Unless Callum or Ivy heard something I haven't?"

"No," Ivy said. "But we hope to have the report soon. Bree, I haven't gotten a good feel for how long he holds each victim before he kills them. Seems to vary quite a bit. But I need to review more documents to be sure."

"Based on the timelines we constructed, it appears that he holds them for less than a day. In one case, as little as four hours. Another, it was almost twelve."

Ryland pulled the five pictures toward him. He carefully studied each one. His eyes held a mixture of sadness and anger when he slid the pictures back to the middle. "I know you collaborated with the FBI on this. But the profile I saw was woefully inadequate."

"The FBI was pretty slammed and couldn't devote the resources we needed. Although we were told if we got another victim, to contact them again and they'd re-evaluate their case load."

Ryland's jaw tightened. "How nice of them."

She shrugged. "To be fair, they were in the middle of a terrorist investigation at the time. I think they did the best they could. We sent information to them and worked with a special agent remotely, through emails and over the phone. He studied the case files and provided suggestions of how to proceed. The seemingly-generic profile they gave us will probably match the suspect once we figure out the killer's identity. But as an investigative tool, it's pretty much worthless."

"Can I see it again?" Ryland asked.

She stood and walked up and down the table, checking the labels on the various boxes and folders, before sorting through one of the boxes at the far end. She pulled out a slim manila folder and gave it to Ryland before resuming her seat.

He pulled out the profile and set it on the table. Ivy and Callum leaned in on either side of him, skimming the contents.

"White male, twenty-five to thirty-five," Ryland said. "That describes about ninety percent of serial killers ever caught."

Bree nodded. "Kind of my take on it too. Since the victims vary in race, I don't even put much stock in the assumption that the killer is white. I think that was a guess, more than anything, based on most serial killers being white males. We should keep an open mind on the killer's race."

She motioned toward the folder. "The profile says he's an organized killer, which again is no surprise since he was meticulous about leaving no forensic clues behind."

Ryland handed the profile to Ivy, who moved to sit beside Callum to read the rest of it.

"Any more questions?" Bree asked. "I think I reviewed all the main points."

"Not yet," Ivy said, "but I reserve the right to ask more as I dig further into the files."

"Of course," Bree said. "I've got time off right now, whether I want it or not. Happy to help in any way that I can."

"Normally," Ryland said, "with cold cases like this, where a serial killer is suspected, we'd try to disprove that the victims are linked. But since the FBI reviewed the case and doesn't dispute the link, we'll accept that premise. Agreed?"

Callum and Ivy, who had finished reading the profile, both nodded.

"Any suggestions you want to offer?" Ivy asked him.

"Re-visit each crime scene as if this is day one and it's a fresh murder," Ryland said. "Focus on victimology. Start with family then build a list of everyone the victims knew—friends, enemies, where they worked. Re-interview key people. Begin to build a timeline. Use the original case as a skeleton but understand some of the bones may be missing or belong to another skeleton altogether. Check cell phone records. Get an expert to perform tool mark analysis on those marked trees, at every scene—including the current one if we can get access to it. Look for the victims' diaries, appointment books. Go through the evidence locker for that and see if their families have old calendars or something that was the victim's that might have more timeline information on them. Even though it doesn't seem useful, go ahead and perform geographical profiling, inclusive of the latest murder. Maybe we can gain an understanding of why the killer may have moved, if it is the same killer."

Bree's head was spinning, listening to everything he was saying. But Ivy and Callum nodded as if it was all part of their normal routine—and maybe it was. They both took notes, just the same.

"Set up social media sites to stir interest by the public," Ryland continued. "Use the Smoky Mountain Slayer name. Sensationalize it. You'll generate a lot more hits that way. Encourage comments and posts of any information about the victims. Oh, and you might want to submit the cases to the Project Cold Case website."

"Project Cold Case?" Bree asked.

"It's a website that encourages people to up-load information about cold cases, to get more eyes on it. You never know when a helpful tip will come along."

She nodded, amazed that he knew about things like that. She'd never heard of it. And she hadn't used social media the way he was describing it. During her time on the Slayer case, she'd searched social media to learn about the victims, not necessarily to generate leads. Ryland was constantly impressing her.

"Callum, let's see if our lab can extract a us-able DNA profile from the evidence in all five killings. Work with Rowan to maintain chain of custody and move the evidence to the lab for testing. Technology changes all the time. Maybe samples were too small to test four and five years ago when the victims were murdered. But touch DNA technology is incredible these days. We might get lucky."

"I'll text him now. We'll start with the first victim since killers tend to make mistakes early on before they perfect their craft. Odds are bet-ter that if there's some DNA to be had, it'll come from that evidence."

"Good thinking," Ryland said. "Ivy, I'd like

you to work with one of our profiler consultants to get a fresh profile, one that includes the latest murder, and one that doesn't—since we don't know yet whether this latest one is related. Maybe our profiler will have better luck at providing something useful. You can compare the profile with any names that come up while looking at each of the victims. Hopefully we'll generate at least a few leads that way."

"You got it." She added to her list on the computer tablet she was using.

"Let's get the team to start reporting status daily, end of day," Ryland said. "And since the team is scattered around, from here to Monroe County, we'll do the status meetings via computer. Callum, can you set the meetings up for, say, the next week, and send the links to everyone?"

"I can get that out before lunch," he said.

"Great. Thanks. Oh, one more thing. This is a side item I'm curious about but really doesn't further our efforts to solve the Slayer case or the recent events. Still, it's bothering me, so I'd appreciate it if one of you could get the ball rolling, maybe pull in Brice or someone else if you need to."

"Of course." Callum said. "What do you need?"

"Palmer has a near-perfect winning record

with his prosecutions. We're talking unheard of percentages, suspiciously high. I want to know what he's doing to make that happen. Maybe pull in a private investigator local to Monroe County who can plug into the town gossip and do some digging. If Palmer's on the up-and-up, fine. If not, I want to know what's going on. If it's something nefarious, I'll present the information to Sheriff Peterson and let him decide what to do about it."

Bree touched Ryland's sleeve. "I appreciate you doing that. It never occurred to me to look into those numbers."

"It's been bugging me since you mentioned it. Might as well see if there's a reason for that."

"I'll take care of it," Callum said. "Anything else?"

"No. I think you and Ivy have more than enough to do right now. Take it a step at a time. If it gets to be too much, ask someone else on the team for help or bring in a consultant to do legwork.

"Bree," Ryland continued, "you'll notice that I allocated our team mostly toward current events. Lance, Faith and Asher are working Patricia Rogers's murder. Trent and Brice are splitting their work between shoring up the safety system on the road out front and working with Gatlinburg PD and your office to investigate how your SUV went off the mountain. And Rowan, our TBI liaison, is working mainly with both of those teams. That's six people working the active investigations, while only Ivy and Callum have been assigned to work specifically on these cold cases." He motioned toward the pictures of the five victims.

"I did notice, actually," she said. "But I'm not complaining. The Rogers murder does appear to be the work of the Slayer. So it makes sense to focus on the one with the freshest evidence. And I appreciate your team trying to find out who ran me off the road and endangered you. If it was on purpose, I want to ensure no one is targeting me and will make another attempt at trying to kill me." She gave a nervous laugh, but no one else laughed.

"That's my number one priority," he said. "I'd like you to continue to stay with me until we figure out who might be after you."

She stared at him, surprised. "I have to go back home soon. My job won't wait forever."

As if on cue, Ivy and Callum moved to the far side of the table and began pulling more files out of the boxes.

Ryland leaned forward, resting his forearms on the table. "I'd prefer you continue to stay with me. It's safer. I can escort you home to pack a bag, if you want. Or take you to a store here to get more clothes. But I really don't think you should be alone. It's too dangerous."

She blinked, not sure what to say. Part of her longed to stay in his cabin, to see him every day. But how much longer could she do that and keep her heart intact? He seemed so perfect for her, in every way. But there was no forever for the two of them. There couldn't be, not with their separate careers two hours apart. And every day they were together would just make it that much harder to leave.

He was watching her intently, waiting for her answer.

She cleared her throat. "I, ah, I'm not sure that—"

His phone buzzed in his pocket. He frowned and checked the screen. "Sorry, I have to take this." He punched the button. "Trent, what've you got?"

By the time Ryland ended the call, Ivy and Callum had moved back to stand with Bree, expectantly watching him. The look on his face and the tone of his voice had alerted all of them that something important had happened.

He closely watched Bree as he updated them. "Trent's in Madisonville. He's been staking out Prosecutor Palmer's house, waiting for him to finally return home. Palmer pulled into his driveway about an hour ago. Bree, he didn't fix his car as you'd feared. The right front part of his bumper is messed up. And there's a white streak of paint across it."

"Son of a… I knew it," Bree said. "I knew he was the one who ran into me." She headed toward the door. "We need to head to Madisonville. I want to be there when Peterson arrests him and—"

"Bree. There's more."

The tone of his voice had her turning around, a feeling of dread shooting through her.

He followed her to the door and stopped in front of her. "Your boss had someone performing surveillance too, one of your detectives. They had Palmer in handcuffs the second he pulled up. Of course, when they showed Palmer the damage to his car, he acted shocked. He claimed someone must have hit it while it was parked on the street. But since he hadn't gone around to the other side, he hadn't noticed the damage."

"Of course he'd say that," Bree said. "I'm just relieved that Sheriff Peterson stepped up. He must have believed me after all to have put Palmer's house under surveillance. Where has Palmer been hiding out all this time?"

He glanced at Ivy and Callum before answering. "I don't know for sure. He claimed he was stressed out over everything that was happening and drove around Tennessee, staying at hotels here and there. Peterson is verifying that. But, Bree, they didn't arrest him because of the bumper. They arrested him because a few hours ago, they found another body in the woods, in Monroe County. And this time, they have video. It shows Palmer driving his car into those woods, then hightailing it out of there just before someone discovered the body. He's been arrested for murder."

Moving to the nearest chair, she slowly sat, nausea making her stomach churn. "Someone else has been killed?"

His eyes were sad as he nodded, then motioned toward the media wall at the end of the room. "Ivy, since you're the closest, would you mind turning on the screen and opening the video link that Trent just sent us? He said the story's blowing up the airwaves in Madisonville right now. Bree, you weren't kidding when you said the press had been stirred up in your county. They're all over this."

The screen turned on. Seconds later, Ivy had the news feed from Madisonville tuned in. The conference room was silent except for the reporter's voice, sensationalizing every little piece of information they had, accurate or not. And behind her, a video kept looping of Prosecutor Palmer being hustled out of a police SUV in handcuffs at the back of the police station.

"I'll hand it to your sheriff," Ryland said. "He did try to keep it quiet. He took him around back instead of doing a perp walk out front."

"He's not the type to do a perp walk, says it's undignified for law enforcement to put someone on parade that way." She shook her head. "Any idea how the reporters got wind of this so fast? Even knowing our press people the way I do, I'm surprised they were at the police station and got those pictures."

"Trent said they…" Ryland motioned toward the TV. "Looks like they're showing that part right now."

They watched in silence as another reporter interviewed the owner of a gas station. He pointed to the woods behind him and told the reporter about a body being found there early this morning, saying that he was in early working on repairs and looked outside.

"He's describing Palmer's car," Bree said. "He was there when it drove into the woods. Is that what happened? He called the police because he saw a suspicious car?"

"That's the story, Trent said. Looks like they're going into those details now."

They watched the rest of the broadcast. When it started over again, as "breaking news," Ivy shut down the feed.

"They didn't mention the victim," Bree said. "Other than that they found a body. Was Trent able to get any information on who was killed? And how?"

"That information has been withheld and Peterson hasn't spoken to him yet."

"At least the family won't hear about their loved one on TV. I hope the autopsy can help ID the victim fast and the family is notified before anyone else figures out who was killed. Do we even know whether it's a male or female?"

"No clue at all."

She stood. "What a mess. My fellow detectives are going to be bombarded by reporters and all kinds of false tips will be called in. It's like the original Slayer case all over again. I need to be there to help them."

Ryland crossed his arms. "I don't suppose I can convince you not to go? To lay low at my place like I was saying earlier? It's better not to take chances with your safety."

"While I appreciate that you want to protect me, I'm not the delicate flower you seem to think I am. I'm going to Madisonville, with or without you."

"Your purse is at the bottom of the ravine, along with your credit cards and ID. That will make it impossible for you to rent a car."

"Blackmail, Ryland? Really?"

"I prefer to call it protection detail. If Palmer isn't the one who tried to kill you—"

"His car is damaged, with white paint on it. He's the one who hit my SUV."

"If he's not," he repeated, "you're still safer staying here. With me."

"Safer or not, I'm not hiding out when my team needs me. And you don't hold all the cards like you think you do. Faith not only brought me clothes and toiletries the other night, she brought me a phone and a UB credit card in case I needed anything else. I've got my personal car at home, with an extra set of keys, cash, and an emergency credit card. I'm all set. I just need a ride to get there. I've already got an account with a driver service. I can call them to pick me up and use my card that's on file." She pulled out her phone as if ready to call for a ride. "Or you can drive me to Madisonville and beg my forgiveness the whole way for trying to dictate where I go and what I do."

Callum laughed, but quickly sobered when Ryland shot him an aggravated look.

"Put the phone away." Ryland's mouth curved in a reluctant grin. "You win. I'll drive you. But I won't be begging your forgiveness. I'll be talking your ear off, trying to talk some sense into you, the whole way there."

Chapter Sixteen

Telling Bree that he'd "talk some sense into her" had apparently not been a good strategy. All Ryland had managed to do was rile her up even more so that the first half of their trip to Madisonville was spent in stony silence with her refusing to say anything.

The second half of the trip, they'd had a vigorous discussion about the case and her role in it. He'd finally gotten her to agree that it made sense for her not to go directly to the sheriff's office to demand an update on the interrogation of Prosecutor Dane Palmer. Of course, that was partly based on him refusing to drive downtown.

Her personal car was in her garage. And since she'd gotten her spare key from her neighbor, there was nothing else Ryland could do to force her to not destroy her own career. But he'd used psychology to stall her for at least a few more minutes. He'd convinced her that if she wanted her boss to take her seriously and not fire her on the spot for ignoring his orders, she might want to change her clothes. Although she certainly looked great to Ryland, he doubted the T-shirt and jeans that Faith had brought her would add much weight to her argument that she was ready to get back to work.

As soon as Bree had disappeared into her bedroom, Ryland had been on the phone with Trent. He'd gotten to Bree's house in record time, probably breaking all the speed limits between the sheriff's office and her home. He'd managed to get here before Bree had come back out. Now he was sitting in the family room, giving Ryland an update.

And the information he had changed everything.

A door closed down the hallway. A few moments later, Bree rounded the corner into the family room, looking even better than the first time Ryland had seen her, which didn't seem possible. Her incredible figure was impossible to disguise, even with loose pleated pants, a dark blouse that covered any hint of cleavage, and a navy-blue blazer that screamed professional businesswoman. It almost made him think he should have put on a suit instead of jeans. Almost. He really hated suits.

She'd done something with her beautiful

blond hair too. It was tamed into some kind of fancy braid. And her fresh makeup emphasized her intriguing hazel eyes and plump pink lips. She was absolutely stunning.

"Hi, Trent." She glanced curiously back and forth between them as she handed the UB credit card to Ryland. "I've grabbed my second set of keys, some cash and my emergency backup credit card from my safe. I don't need the UB card now." She moved past him and sat in the chair facing him and Trent on the couch. "What's going on? Trent, are you heading downtown with us?"

"No. He's not," Ryland said, finally finding his voice. "We're not going downtown."

"I'll, uh, just head out," Trent said. "I've got a few more things to look into."

"Text me any updates," Ryland told him. "If I don't hear from you, I'll see you on the video chat at tonight's status call."

Trent nodded. "Bree, I'll see you around."

With that, he was gone. Bree turned a puzzled look to Ryland. "What's going on? I don't want to miss Palmer's interrogation."

"Your boss ordered you not to even think about the case. It's better to let him wonder whether you're following orders rather than show up and prove you're not. You did say you wanted to keep your job. Has that changed?"

She frowned. "What's changed is that the man who tried to kill me has been arrested. I want to see him, ask him that all-important question—why."

"Maybe he was mad about how you interviewed him at UB headquarters. Or maybe he was worried you were too clever, that you knew the Slayer cases so well that having Palmer as the primary suspect would make all the puzzle pieces come together in your mind. Or maybe he'll never answer that question. Regardless, it's not like your boss will give you a chance to ask him. You're the victim. Victims don't interrogate the people accused of hurting them."

She started to argue again, but he held up his hands in a placating gesture.

"You asked me why Trent was here. He just came from the sheriff's office and managed to get one of your coworkers to give him some information. I really think you want to hear this before risking your career to demand an audience you're not going to get."

She let out a frustrated breath. "All right. Update me on whatever Trent found out. Then if you don't want to go with me to the office, I'll take my own car."

He motioned toward the couch.

She rolled her eyes and sat. "Okay. What's this important information I need to know?"

He sat beside her, facing her, resting his right arm across the back of the couch. "The story that Trent got is that Palmer insists he's not the one who drove into the woods this morning where the body was found."

"Well, of course he's denying it. But he's on video. The gas station owner on the newscast said he saw him, that it's him on camera."

"You're right. His surveillance camera clearly shows the license plate. It's been verified with the DMV records. Since your boss was already on the alert about Palmer coming back, when the plate was run, he was called. That's how this all came together so fast."

She frowned. "And Palmer? The witness didn't mention him. Was Palmer on the video?"

"The driver is captured on the video. I'm told he looks like Palmer."

"*Looks* like him? They aren't sure?"

"The video quality isn't that good, bad enough to potentially give a jury reasonable doubt. They need more evidence."

"Okay, well, the bumper damage is evidence of what he did to me. And they should be able to work up a timeline of when he left wherever he's been staying versus when he got to his house."

"I'm sure they will. Trent's trying to get that information to work the timeline from our end."

She thought about it a moment. "The proof is in the license plate. It's on video. And since it was Palmer who was driving his car when he got home this morning, not someone else, he's the killer."

"Back up a minute," he said. "It sounds damning. But if someone had told you a week ago that Palmer was a murderer, and that he'd try to send someone careening over a cliff, what would you have said? Honestly. After knowing him for years."

She stared at him a long moment, then looked away. "I'd have said they were crazy. But that doesn't change the facts. How many people are shocked when they find out their next-door neighbor, the nice, quiet guy, goes on a rampage and takes out a bunch of people at a shopping mall with an AK-47? It happens."

"You're right. It absolutely does. And I'm not saying that Palmer is innocent. But what if he is?"

She slowly turned to look at him again. "Innocent until proven guilty is the most basic principal in our justice system, and I think it's the most important guiding principal we have. I'd rather a killer went free than send an innocent person to prison."

He smiled and took her hand in his. "I'm with you on that. It's the core belief that guides everything I do in my job. So with that in mind, I'm going to throw out some what-ifs. Okay?"

She crossed her arms, obviously not happy, but she was trying to keep an open mind. And he loved that about her. "Go ahead."

"What if Palmer's wallet really was stolen from his car? What if he really did go to Gatlinburg to buy his mother a birthday present, but never found what he wanted, so he didn't realize his wallet was stolen? What if he really did hear the police chatter on the radio when you and I discovered the body, and he came up Prescott Mountain out of curiosity and maybe even ego, thinking he might be able to offer theories or suggestions? What if it wasn't his car up on the mountain, and he's not the one who slammed into your bumper?"

Her mouth tightened, but she didn't say anything.

"And finally, what if he really did go straight home from wherever he was staying this morning and didn't stop off in the woods to dump a body? If everything I just said is true, then what conclusions does that lead you to make?"

She shook her head. "That he'd be the unluckiest guy in the world, which of course is ludicrous. Someone else would have to have a car just like his and is driving it around to the same places he's going, making it look like he's a killer. But that's not possible since the video shows his car in the woods. Same make, model, color, and with his license plate. Don't forget that part."

"I haven't." He pulled his phone out, punched up the picture that Trent had sent him, and handed the phone to her. "Swipe to view the last three pictures on my phone."

She took it and studied each of them. "It's Palmer's car."

"Are you sure?"

She frowned and studied the pictures more closely. "Same make, model, color. The front bumper is mangled with white paint streaked across it. Is this plate the same as Palmer's?"

"It is."

"Okay. Well, then, it's definitely his car. But I don't recognize the surroundings. That dilapidated wooden fence behind the car isn't the brick fence that surrounds Palmer's neighborhood. Where was the picture taken?"

"A junkyard outside of town."

Her gaze shot to his. "When?"

"This morning, shortly after Palmer was arrested. Trent found it. On a hunch, based on some past experiences with other cases, he called around to all the junkyards in town to see if the car had been taken there. One of the owners checked and called him back."

She shook her head. "I don't understand. Peterson would have had Palmer's car impounded downtown, not sent to a junkyard."

"Palmer's car *was* impounded. Still is. Trent verified it. He checked the VIN on both vehicles and they're different. This isn't Palmer's car."

"I don't…that doesn't make sense. Palmer's car was damaged when he pulled up in his driveway. That has to be his car."

"Remember he said it was parked on the street. It is possible that someone damaged it while it was on the street, and he never saw it."

"He'd have heard it. Or someone else would have. It takes a lot of force to crumple a bumper."

"Good point. Maybe our copycat stole the car while Palmer was sleeping, drove it somewhere else, took a sledgehammer to it and painted the bumper white. Then he brought it back and parked it right where Palmer had left it."

"Sounds really farfetched."

"And yet, it's the only way I can think of to explain how we have two different cars that look identical and have the same damage."

"I'm open to someone framing Palmer," she said. "But I'm trying to understand how that would work. Let's say the guy who jumped in front of your Rover wasn't Palmer. How did he know to wear jeans and a white shirt the same day Palmer did?"

"Maybe he keeps surveillance on him. He may have been in Palmer's house to find out what outfits he has, and he's bought the same for himself. So every day, he dresses however Palmer does that day. And every day, he's trying to do something to make Palmer look bad. Maybe most of the time, there isn't anything he can do. But he's patient, and sticks to the plan."

She rubbed her hands up and down her arms. "Okay, that's super creepy, sneaking into his house, copying his wardrobe, and following him around for days or weeks, maybe longer."

"Imagine the kind of person who would do all that? If he does exist, and he's been keeping an eye on Palmer and mimicking him and has this disguise to look like him, it becomes plausible that he decides to plant the wallet and hopes to lead people to the grave at some point."

"Not just some people," she said. "He was counting on it being an investigator familiar with the case. He would have assumed that you knew about the gouges on the trees."

"Right. I can't imagine him planning for Palmer to show up in the woods the day we found the grave. The killer lucked out when that happened. But he planted the wallet, regardless, to throw suspicion on Palmer whenever the body was discovered."

"I guess that would work." She sat there a few moments, then clasped her hands tightly in her lap. "There's another option." Her voice was quiet, reserved.

"What would that be?"

"Back to the theory that everything points to Palmer because he *is* the Slayer, not because someone else is framing him."

"But the duplicate cars—"

"I'll get to that. Hear me out. There's no DNA, a lack of forensic clues in any of the original five Slayer killings. That's not an easy feat. It had to be done by someone who is smart, cunning, controlled, and plans everything out. Like Palmer. Maybe the gap in the killings is because the Slayer—Palmer—felt the heat of the investigation and was worried we might catch him, so he backed off. But he's a sociopath, so he can't stop forever. When he heard that Unfinished Business was going to look into his killings, his ego wouldn't let him ignore that. He wants to prove he's the bigger, badder guy, that he can outsmart UB. So he starts killing again both to confuse UB and to provide a diversion, to give investigators an alternate theory about what's happening. He's taunting UB. But he also wants to make a statement, let

Monroe County know they can't catch him. So he tries running me off the cliff, as a message, basically, that no one can catch him."

"Bree, this is really elaborate pie-in-the-sky stuff. It doesn't make sense."

"What part of being a sociopath makes sense?"

He shrugged. "I don't see how you can argue any of this. It's based on conjecture, not facts."

"I think we've already established that you and I look at investigations differently. That doesn't mean a theory I come up with isn't ultimately true."

"You're right, and I don't mean to say that my way is the only way—"

"Really? You sure about that?" she teased.

He grimaced. "Sorry. I can be a bit overbearing sometimes, my way or no way. I'll allow that your way of investigating can be just as valuable as mine, all right?"

"Can I get that in writing?"

He laughed. "I just want to mention the two cars again. How does your theory explain that?"

"Alibi. Think about it. It's brilliant, really."

He stared at her a long moment, then nodded. "I think I know where you're headed with this. But go ahead."

"All right. Assuming Palmer's the killer, he left the wallet at the grave to make it look like someone is framing him. And he stored a second car, just like his, in the back of a junkyard in case he needs a way to point to someone setting him up. I'm guessing he used the backup car for hauling bodies, so a cadaver dog wouldn't get a scent hit on his own car. That's probably the original reason he got two cars."

"Ah. Good theory there. That would make sense, if he's setting up an elaborate alibi. Keep going."

"Okay. Where's the junkyard in relation to where he dumped the body?"

"Not far. Maybe a quarter mile," he said.

"He dumps the body, switches cars so he's in the clean car. When the second car is discovered, cadaver dogs will indicate that's the car that hauled bodies, not Palmer's car. As you indicated, the vehicle identification number proves which car is his personal car. I'm guessing the second car was stolen at some point?"

"Trent is trying to find out. But I certainly can't see someone leaving legit registration back to themselves, so stolen works."

"No one is ever going to believe that Palmer would steal a car and kill someone, not without hard evidence. We're talking DNA. It's like a get-out-of-jail-free card. He can do whatever he wants, setting himself up to look like someone is out to get him. And I'll bet the only DNA the police will find is in that second car, which isn't Palmer's car. With his reputation, his standing in the community, there just might be enough reasonable doubt to get him off."

"Are you playing devil's advocate?" he asked. "Or do you honestly believe everything you just said actually happened?"

She held her hands out and shrugged. "Doesn't matter what I believe. The facts are what matters. All I'm saying is that the facts can be interpreted in two completely different ways. Either Palmer is sadistically smart and playing with everyone, having a grand old time to prove how he can outsmart them, or he's truly innocent and someone else is setting him up, as you said. Keep in mind, if I can come up with a complex yet explainable alternative to Palmer being the killer, so can a defense attorney."

Ryland swore. "You're right about that. And I told Trent to let Peterson know about the second car. So if Palmer is using the two cars as a way to cast reasonable doubt that he's being framed, we just did half the work for him by alerting the police."

They both sat in silence for a few moments. Then Bree said, "We need more facts to point us in the right direction. The question is, where do we get those facts? What do we do next in order to figure out whether Palmer is innocent or guilty?"

"Old-fashioned investigative work. We need to really dig into Palmer's life, past and present. We need to find out if there's anyone who hates him so much that they'd resort to murder and a frame-up to destroy his life. Knowing him, is there anyone you can think of who might fit that category?"

She chuckled. "You're kidding, right? Try everyone he's put in prison over the years."

"I'm not sure I agree with that. If someone's trying to frame him, they're risking everything to do it. And they have to be willing to kill other people, collateral damage, just to frame Palmer. I doubt the vast majority of people he's put away fall into that category. We'll have to talk to family, friends, coworkers, anyone we can to build a picture and come up with those potential names. And we check with Palmer himself to see if anyone has ever threatened him, someone he takes seriously and was or is concerned about. It could very well be someone he put in prison, who has since gotten out and blames him for whatever they lost while in prison. A lot of those guys lose everything, even with a short stint behind bars. Their families abandon them. Possessions get confiscated, sold. Houses are foreclosed on. The careers they've built are destroyed. Especially if, God forbid, they were innocent and sent to prison. That's enough to warp anyone's mind."

She arched a brow. "And turn them into a killer?"

He shrugged. "I suppose it's possible. But once again, we're making leaps. Let's start at the source."

"Palmer."

He nodded. "Somehow, I've got to get your boss to let me question him."

She slowly shook her head. "No. He won't let a civilian near him. I have to question him."

"Peterson ordered you not to work any cases. We have to find another way to get the information that we need. You know how things work at the sheriff's office. And you know the people who work there. How can you get the information from Palmer without sacrificing your career to get it?"

Chapter Seventeen

The bell tinkled over the doorway to the little café, causing Ryland to look toward the door from the booth he and Bree had chosen at the back. A young woman with auburn hair stepped in, looking around as if she was trying to find someone.

"Is that her?" Ryland asked.

Bree glanced up from her menu and looked over her shoulder. "Ah, no. Melanie's closer to forty than twenty, and she's got brown hair."

"Are you sure she's coming?"

"I'm sure. She's wanted this for a long time."

"This? What are you talking about?"

"In exchange for getting us the information we needed, I made a deal to…" The bell tinkled again. She looked back and waved. "That's her."

The woman started down the long aisle toward them.

"I don't think you mentioned which detective she's dating."

"And I won't. The fewer people who know, the better. I don't want to get him in trouble." She rose as Melanie stopped beside their booth. "Mel, hey. This is investigator Ryland Beck. He works for Unfinished Business, like I told you."

He stood and shook her hand. "Ms., ah, I don't think I got your last name."

"Her name is Mel. That's all you need to know," Bree said. "Ignore him, Mel. He's not comfortable not knowing every little detail. Thanks so much for agreeing to help. Have a seat." She slid across the booth to make room.

Melanie gave Ryland an uncertain smile as he sat across from her and Bree. She warily glanced around the café. "I'll just leave this with you. I have to get back to the office." She took a manila envelope out of her purse and set it on the table. She leaned in close to Bree. "The interview was on the record. Peterson had no problem with him going in and asking Palmer your follow-up questions. I only printed out the transcript of the part you asked about."

Bree squeezed the other woman's hand. "Thank you so much, Mel. This will really help with our investigation."

"I still don't know why you aren't working it officially with the others. But I won't pry." She looked around, as if searching for something. "Where is it?"

Ryland frowned. "Where's what?"

"It's on the back porch, wrapped up and safe. The gate's unlocked."

Mel's face flushed with excitement. "I can't wait. I'll stop by on my way back to the office. I don't want to risk someone else discovering it outside. Thanks, Bree. You don't know how long I've wanted this."

Bree's expression was a bit pained. "You have great taste. Hope you enjoy it."

"Oh, I will, I will. Good luck with your investigation. Nice to meet you, Mr. Beck."

"You too, Ms...."

"Holland." She put her hand on her mouth. "Oh, oops. It's so hard to keep a secret. Forget I said that." She hurried down the aisle and out of the café.

"Why did you do that?" Bree asked. "You knew she wanted to remain anonymous, or as much as possible anyway."

He rolled his eyes. "She works in the sheriff's office and dates one of the detectives. She has access to the records and can print transcripts of interrogations. Five-four, a little on the heavy side, about forty, with shoulder-length curly brown hair. Oh, and her first name is Melanie but I'm assuming that everyone calls her Mel, since you do. With all that, do you honestly think I couldn't have figured out her last name? Asking was easier, and it worked. Besides, her picture's probably in that stack of photos you already gave me, with her name written on the back."

She laughed. "You're right. It is. So much for *me* keeping secrets." She took a sip of her Pepsi.

"At least now I know why you took that painting down from over your couch before we left and set it on the back porch. What I don't understand is why you agreed to give it up in exchange for information from Palmer. We could have gotten it another way without you losing something you so obviously loved."

"You could tell I loved it?"

"Are you kidding? There were tears in your eyes as you told her it was on the back porch. It's not too late. We can head over there, stop her before she takes it. I've got access to a substantial petty cash fund at UB. Grayson would consider it payment for services rendered if I bribe your friend to forgo the painting."

"Ha. Trust me. That wouldn't happen. She's wanted that since the day she came over for a dinner I put on for us detectives and their significant others. She's an art lover, like me. And almost drooled on my floor wanting it. I consider it a small price to pay if it helps us figure out what's going on."

"What's so special about the painting? I mean, it's pretty and all. But it's just a landscape."

Her eyes widened. "Just a landscape? That's like saying a Lamborghini is just a car."

He grinned. "Consider me schooled. This is where I admit I know close to nothing about art."

"I won't waste our time trying to go into the history of the painter and that particular painting. Suffice it to say it means a lot to me. I practically starved for a whole year to save for it because it was coming up at auction. The fact that I got it was a small miracle. What made it more special is that it was a gift to my mom, who absolutely cherished it. I inherited it after she and my daddy passed within a few months of each other. It always reminds me of them, and makes me smile when I see it." Her mouth tightened in a firm line. "Or it did. It's going to be hard to get used to not seeing it hanging over the couch anymore."

She grabbed the manila envelope and worked at opening the seal.

"I'm sure I can buy it back—"

"Let it go, Ryland. Consider it my first real contribution to the case. Let's see if it was worth the sacrifice." She pulled out the small stack of papers that were inside. "Six pages. That's a lot of names to have to look into." She quickly scanned them. "Double-spaced. That helps. Fewer names to whittle down." She shook her head. "Still a lot to dig through. Looks like Palmer rambled a bit. He listed fifteen or twenty people who might want to frame him."

"Can I see it?"

She handed him the pages and took another sip of her drink.

Ryland snapped pictures with his phone's camera as he scanned the interview excerpt, singling out the names Palmer had mentioned.

When the waitress stopped by to see if they needed anything else, Bree thanked her and said their lunch was delicious and they'd be leaving soon.

As the waitress moved to another booth, Ryland attached the pictures to a text.

"What are you doing with those?" Bree asked. "Sending them to someone else?"

"Callum. I asked him to do a quick check on the names, see if he can get addresses, or at least last known locations."

"How many names did you find in the transcript?"

"You were close. Sixteen. Those are the only

people. Once we interview Palmer's family and friends, we may add a few more people who hate him to that list. But it's a start. Are you ready to go?"

"Definitely. Where to? Back to my place?"

"Until we solve this thing and can be sure who rammed your SUV, I still think you should stay with me in Gatlinburg. So, yeah, let's head back so you can pack a suitcase."

"Works for me. Now that I have this information from Palmer, I'm okay not sticking around in Madisonville. Especially since I'll be with a man who risked his life, in spite of his phobia about heights, to save me. I'll never be able to repay that debt. Thank you, Ryland."

He grimaced at the mention of his fear of heights as he escorted her outside. "Stop thanking me. That would be a great start at repayment. Unless you want to thank me the same way you did at my cabin." Although he was teasing, he wouldn't stop her if she wanted to kiss him again. *He* sure as hell wanted to kiss *her*.

Bree's face flushed and she cleared her throat. "Um, we can explore that later, after the case is resolved." She glanced up at him. "And then maybe you'll tell me what happened."

"What happened?"

"To make you afraid of heights."

His throat tightened. "One day. Maybe." But he doubted it. That wasn't something he liked talking about to anyone. The only reason his teammates knew about it was because they'd all been together when he'd fainted once before. And then Trent had dug into his background to find out the cause of his fear. He'd hated Trent for it at the time. But they'd gotten past that and had become the very best of friends.

He and Bree had just pulled into her driveway when his phone buzzed. He cut the engine and checked the screen. "That was fast. Callum already found six of the people on the list. They're all in the same place."

"Madisonville, I'd imagine."

"The Riverbend Maximum Security prison in Nashville."

"Oh. Well, we can mark those six off since they couldn't be involved in framing Palmer." She grabbed her purse, ready to get out of the car.

"Actually, I'd kind of like to talk to them."

She settled back against the seat. "Why?"

"He put them away. They've got strong motives to hate him. And he obviously agrees or he wouldn't have mentioned them. There are plenty of cases where people in prison masterminded murder outside the prison walls. We can explore this first group fairly quickly, see if there are any red flags that go up. If one of them seems to be hiding something, we can dig deeper and see if they could be involved, see who their contacts are. All it takes is one good friend or a family member outside of prison to carry out their plans. We just have to follow the bread crumbs."

"Okay. Not something I'd have necessarily thought to do," she said. "But I'm game. Send me the six you're talking about and I'll notify the prison, find out if or when we can have access to the prisoners. If they're due in court for an appeal or something like that, they might not be available for an interview. But I'd think at least one or two should be capable of accepting visitors, today if the prison will be flexible since I'm law enforcement. Family or press would never be able to do a last-minute visit. It usually takes weeks to get permission for a visit to someone like these on the list, the maximum security prisoners."

"Sending you the list now." He pressed some buttons on his phone. "Done."

When she read all of the names, she grimaced. "Never thought I'd apply to visit any of these creeps after what they did. Silas Gerloff, that road rage guy I told you about. Dan Smith, the workplace violence guy. Wait, why is the child murderer, Nancy Compadre, on this list? The profile says the killer is a man."

"The profile of the original Slayer murders. We don't have a profile yet for these most recent murders, and I don't feel we're in a situation where we can cross someone off our potential suspect list without talking to them first. Or at least speaking to someone who knows them."

"Point taken. She stays. Let's see, oh, this one isn't in prison, unless he was sent back for something else."

"Who?" he asked.

"Liam Kline. He's the pedophile I told you about earlier. Well, at least, he was convicted as a pedophile. But his conviction was overturned. He was released about a year ago."

"You never told me why his conviction was overturned. Do you know?"

She grimaced. "Mistakes were made with the handling of evidence. Kline was convicted of possessing child pornography on his computer at work. He was originally sentenced to twenty years. Kline's lawyer appealed and argued that the prosecution had exculpatory evidence that proved another guy at his workplace had access to his computer. And he's right. The guy did have access. But Kline didn't know that, certainly not during the original trial. The second guy was a janitor working night shift. He was also a pedophile, with a prior conviction, easily found if you search the state's sexual predator database. Kline couldn't adequately explain the porn on the computer in his office since he didn't know of anyone who could access it. It was only through discovery after the conviction that the lawyer working on the appeal was able to find out the prosecution team had all of that information and never gave it to the defense."

"Are you saying that Palmer knowingly convicted a man he knew was innocent?"

"No. That's what Kline's lawyer says. My view is that Palmer had too many cooks in the kitchen. The junior prosecutors each had a little piece of the overall puzzle in their files. But they didn't put it together and realize what they had. The evidence wasn't logged properly and wasn't given to the defense during discovery."

"I find that hard to believe," he said. "As organized as you say Palmer is, how could he make a mistake like that?"

"He didn't. His team did. Big difference."

"Okay, okay. I see your point. Maybe Palmer didn't convict an innocent man on purpose. But that doesn't make it any less devastating to the guy who was labeled a pedo. How long was he in prison?"

She cleared her throat. "Three years."

Ryland swore. "Okay. We definitely need to talk to this Kline guy. He's got motive and opportunity since he's a free man. I don't know if he has the money to purchase a look-alike car and buy elaborate disguises to make himself look and dress like Palmer, but—"

"Oh, he does. He took the city, and Palmer, to civil court. And won. Millions, although I'm not sure of the exact amount."

"That probably went a long way toward making amends. Three years, millions of dollars. A lot of people might think he got a good deal. We should look into him anyway. What happened to Palmer? Did he get some kind of reprimand on his record? Have to pay civil fines to Kline?"

"I honestly don't know. If he did, it was kept hush-hush. If you can trust the news reports, Kline signed some kind of nondisclosure agreement where he couldn't say anything about the exact amount of the settlement or any repercussions to the prosecutor's office. The only reason I know the amount was in the millions is because of scuttlebutt at the office. One of the clerks involved in typing up the agreement told a friend who told a friend."

He smiled. "Kind of like Mel Holland. Secrets aren't easy to keep. They always come out."

"Seems that way. Let's head inside. Submitting this request to visit the five others in prison is too hard to do on my phone. I'll use my laptop."

"While you're doing that, and packing a suitcase, I'll see if I can get a current address for Liam Kline."

Chapter Eighteen

For Ryland's sake, Bree wished the ex Mrs. Kline would have asked her and Ryland into her Gatlinburg mountain home. But instead, she'd invited them to sit at the table on her wraparound porch—a porch that had an excellent view of the town of Gatlinburg, a few thousand feet below. The few times that Ryland had made the mistake of glancing toward the railing, he'd quickly looked away, his face going pale. Now he steadfastly focused on whoever was talking, or tapped notes into his phone app.

"Thank you again for agreeing to meet with us," Bree said. "It wasn't easy finding you since you've changed your last name and moved to Gatlinburg. I'm so grateful that your husband's lawyer was able to give a message to your lawyer and that you called me back. If we have follow-up questions after today's visit, I hope you won't mind if Ryland or I call you directly? We've both saved your number in our phones.

But if you'd prefer we go through the lawyers again, we'll delete your number."

"You can call me all you want. As to whether I'll answer next time, we'll see. You said you're working on some type of investigation and needed to talk to me about Liam. That got my curiosity going. I can't imagine him being in trouble again. What's going on?"

"We just need to talk to him about a case."

"I told you over the phone that I don't know where he is."

Bree nodded, not willing to admit that she and Ryland were skeptical of that claim. That's why they were here. To try to pressure her for his address. The lawyer route, trying to get his address that way, had gone nowhere.

"Understood," Bree said. "We'll try contacting him through his lawyer, like we did you. But we'd like some background information for our discussion with him. Can you tell me how long you've lived in Gatlinburg?"

"I sure don't see where that matters. But I didn't understand the odd questions the detectives asked me when Liam was arrested either." She shrugged. "I guess my kids and I have been here a little over three years now. It was impossible to stay in Madisonville. The press wasn't exactly kind to my family after Liam was charged, even worse during the trial.

They speculated, openly, that maybe I'd known what he was doing and had covered for him. My children were bullied at school. All our friends turned their backs on us. I tried to be the supportive wife, to believe in my husband and protect my family as best I could. But the things that came out during the trial…" She shook her head. "It was awful. Once the verdict came in, and he was found guilty, I started looking for a new place, landed here."

Her hand shook as she pushed her light brown bangs out of her eyes. "Liam appealed, of course. He sent me letters from prison, proclaiming his innocence. But I… I didn't believe him. It's horrible to not be able to believe in your own husband, even more horrible years later when his appeal wins and the new evidence proves, beyond any doubt, that he was innocent all along."

Her eyes were bright with unshed tears. "My husband deserved my support and got none. It's a regret I'll have to live with the rest of my life. But there's no fixing it now. Once that pedophile label is put on someone, it sticks. There are people who will always believe he's guilty, that he got off on a technicality, without even looking at the evidence and realizing he was exonerated. I remember what it was like for me, for my boys, to live under that stigma.

I'll always love Liam. But I can't live like that again. I just can't."

Bree gave the woman what she hoped was a commiserating look. But even though she could empathize with what she and her children had gone through, she felt even worse for what Liam Kline had suffered. The people he loved the most in this world, the people he desperately needed to believe in him, didn't. They'd turned away, leaving him completely alone as he was sent to prison, knowing that the pedophile label put him in terrible jeopardy with other inmates and would likely force him to be in solitary for his own protection.

Ryland gave her a sympathetic look too and rested his forearms on the table. "Are your sons still here with you?"

Her expression brightened. "Oh, yes. Larry and Lyle are too young to be on their own. Although, hard to believe, Larry just started high school this year. Lyle's still in middle school. That's where they are right now, at school. I'm fortunate to work from home. That's why I was able to meet with you after you called." Her smile faded. "I'm sorry I can't help you as far as giving you an address for Liam. I truly don't know where he's living now. You should work with his lawyer to get that information."

"We will, for sure. He didn't contact you

when he got out of prison? Does he not know where you live?"

"I've never revealed my new name or address to him. But he still contacts me, through our lawyers sometimes as I already said, but mainly through email. I use a new account for my other correspondences. But I've kept my old account open, for Liam's emails. I don't have the heart to shut it down completely. But I quit reading and responding to him long ago. It's too depressing."

"What about child support?" Bree asked. "It's rumored he got millions in the civil case he won against the city. Did you get a judgment against him for support?"

She raised her chin. "I did. I know it sounds bad that I don't communicate with him but I take his money. But they are his children. They deserve some of the good things in life too, and he can afford it."

"No judgment here," Bree said. "But if he's paying child support, how does that money get to you?"

"Wire transfer. Our lawyers set it up."

"And visitation? How is that handled? A third party? Supervised by the courts at a neutral location?"

Her face reddened. "There is no visitation. I've been fighting him on that for the past six months. When he first got out of prison, he didn't talk about shared custody. But now he's going after me in court, trying to force me to let him see them. There's no way I'll ever let that happen. I have to protect my sons."

Bree straightened in her chair. "Protect them? Are you afraid of him, Mrs. Kline?"

Her hesitation told the story. The woman was definitely afraid of her former husband. What Bree wanted to know was why.

"Mrs. Kline?" she pressed. "Did your husband ever hurt you or your children?"

"What? No, no. Of course not. Liam was a good man, a good husband and father. It's just…" She twisted her hands together on top of the table.

"I know this is hard," Bree said. "But it's important."

Her eyes narrowed. "I don't think you ever explained what case you're working on. You said you had questions about Liam, that he might be able to help you. But I don't see how. What's this about?"

Bree didn't want to say that Liam Kline was a potential suspect in some murders. He'd been falsely convicted once, and lost his family, his livelihood, his reputation—everything—because of it. She couldn't risk telling his ex-wife about their investigation without also risking that rumors would spread and his name would be whispered about as a suspect in serial killings. Without hard facts to implicate him, they were simply on a fishing expedition. And there were plenty of other names on Prosecutor Palmer's list of people to look into. Bree gave Ryland a *help me* look.

He smiled at Mrs. Kline. "It would be unethical to discuss the investigation. But I assure you, we're hoping Mr. Kline can help us. His name came up with several others as someone who may be able to point us toward a suspect."

Bree nodded, impressed with how he'd framed it. Everything he'd said was true. But he made it sound as if Kline wasn't under suspicion in any way.

Mrs. Kline relaxed against her chair, apparently willing to accept Ryland's explanation. "I really can't help you with an address. But you can get a message to him through his lawyer. Obviously you already have *his* contact info. I sincerely hope Liam can help you, but I wouldn't count on him wanting to. Liam is…different than he used to be. He's changed. That's why I don't want him to visit with the children."

Bree stared at her, well aware that Ryland seemed just as surprised as her. It sounded as if Mrs. Kline had contradicted her earlier statement that she hadn't seen Liam since his conviction.

"Liam is different now?" Ryland asked. "What makes you say that? I thought you hadn't seen him in years."

She stiffened. "I didn't lie, Mr. Beck. I haven't seen Liam since the day they took him out of the courtroom in chains. But I read enough of his emails in the beginning of his prison sentence to see him…change. He was such a kind, sweet, handsome man. Everything I'd ever wanted. Even knowing he was guilty…"

She cleared her throat. "Even *believing* he was guilty, in the years before his appeal proved his innocence, I had a hard time ignoring him. Love isn't a faucet you can just turn off and on. It broke my heart reading about his suffering, the horrible things that happened to him in prison. What they did to him, well, it would break anyone. It certainly broke Liam. He became harder, more…coarse. There was a darkness in his words. Hate. That's what scared me, Detective Clark. Realizing the man I'd loved was gone, and in his place was a bitter stranger. It got so bad I had to stop reading his emails. And that darkness is why I'll fight to my last breath to keep custody of my kids, and make sure they never see the man their father has become. I'd rather they remember him the way he was."

Bree leaned forward. "You said what happened to him would break anyone. What did you mean?"

As if looking deep within herself, she stared out over the mountains, a faraway look in her eyes. "My lawyer explained to me that pedophiles are often placed in solitary confinement for their own protection, or even in a special ward in the prison to keep them away from the general population. I guess the inmates have some kind of twisted code. You can rape and murder all day long and they treat you like a hero. Harm a child, and you've crossed some kind of line. I don't know why Liam wasn't immediately put in solitary. Maybe it was an honest mistake, an oversight. Or maybe the guards wanted to see first whether he'd be okay without separating him from everyone else. They put him in a cell with a killer. He was attacked before the end of the first day."

She ran her hands up and down the light jacket she was wearing. "My lawyer sent me a picture, an update on what had happened. I guess he felt I should know since Liam doesn't have any family besides me and the kids." She shivered, swallowed. "I told him not to share anything else about Liam again. I couldn't handle seeing anything that…awful. It still gives me nightmares."

When she went silent, Bree glanced at Ryland. He shrugged, not sure what to do either. Finally, Bree cleared her throat, to get her attention. "Mrs. Kline—"

"His face looked like it had been put through a meat grinder." Mrs. Kline continued to stare out past the mountains, but her entire body was shaking. "The things they did to him." A single tear slid down her cheek. "It's a miracle he survived. But after…after what they did, he didn't even look…human."

"I'm so sorry about your husband," Bree said. "For what he suffered."

She turned to look at Bree, a single tear rolling down her cheek. "*Ex*-husband. I'm sorry, but I can't help you. We're finished here." With that, she went into the house, closing the door behind her with a loud click.

Bree and Ryland didn't speak again until they were sitting in his Rover. He started the engine and got the heater running, but instead of returning to UB headquarters where they'd been earlier, setting up the meeting with Mrs. Kline, he seemed lost in thought, staring out the windshield.

Bree sat back too, grateful for the reprieve.

She wasn't ready to face anyone else at UB just yet. She felt too bruised, raw, and terribly sad.

Ryland was the one who finally spoke. "She said her husband was broken, filled with hate. If anything could turn a good man bad, what Liam Kline suffered would do it. We have to keep him on our potential suspect list."

"You're right," she said. "He seems like our most likely suspect at this point. But I hate it. I hate that an innocent man had his life ruined, his face…the person he sees in the mirror every day—destroyed. And we're going to make it worse by asking him if he's the guy killing people. And trying to frame Palmer." She shook her head. "It's awful."

"It has to be done. We can't ignore him because we empathize with what he's been through."

"I know," she said. "I know. It just really sucks."

"I won't argue that." He glanced at the digital display in the dash. "It's not time yet for the status call, and we still have plenty of daylight. Have you heard back from the prison yet about our request?"

She pulled out her phone and scrolled through her emails. Most were junk mail, but one had an official look about it. It was from the prison.

"We're in luck. Two are available today, the others are available tomorrow. I just need to confirm what time we'll get there so they can prepare."

He glanced at the clock again. "Riverbend's about four hours from here, give or take. We'd arrive after dark. Will they let us interview them that late?"

"Only one way to find out." She called the number from the email. A few minutes later, she ended the call. "Since it'll be so late, they're limiting it to one today. But we can still interview the others tomorrow, starting bright and early at eight. My suitcase is still in the back, but what about you? Do we need to go to your house first and get you a suitcase?"

"My go-bag's in the back. I'm all set." He pulled out onto the road. "Which dirtbag do we get the pleasure of talking to tonight?"

"Silas Gerloff. The road rage killer."

Chapter Nineteen

The sound of chains rattling in the outer corridor was soon followed by the sight of four prison guards escorting Silas Gerloff toward the interview room. Ryland noted the shackles on Gerloff's ankles and wrists and the heavy length of chain connecting them. He glanced at Bree, who was wide-eyed and appeared to be just as surprised as he was.

He leaned in close. "That's a lot of guards and chains for a guy who murdered one person in a road rage incident."

"I was thinking the same thing. Maybe he's done some really bad things inside the prison walls that we don't know about."

"Here he comes."

"Mr. Beck, Detective Clark," one of the guards called out. "Back up against the wall. Do not approach the prisoner."

Bree hesitated.

"Come on," Ryland whispered. He took her

hand and pulled her with him about ten feet from the table where they'd been sitting in the middle of the room.

"Clear," the guard called out. "Open the door."

An electronic buzz sounded, and the heavy barred door slowly slid back, metal screeching as it cleared the opening and sank into a slot in the wall.

"Guard number two, see to the chairs."

One of the guards hurried into the room. He picked up the chair that Ryland had been sitting in and placed it in front of him, then did the same with Bree's chair, leaving only one chair at the heavy steel table, which was bolted into the floor.

"Ready, sir," the guard said, waiting beside the table.

The lead guard, standing behind Gerloff, barked out another order. "Prisoner, move forward. To the table, then halt and sit. No sudden moves."

Gerloff shuffled forward in his orange jumpsuit, chains clinking and swaying. Ryland was amazed he could even walk beneath their weight. There certainly wasn't any danger that Gerloff would make a sudden move. The dark-haired man couldn't be more than five and a half feet tall, and probably weighed about a buck forty. But he looked solid, his muscles well-defined, at least what muscles Ryland could see beneath his tattoos. They covered every inch of his arms, even the backs of his hands and knuckles. But they stopped just beneath his chin. There were none on his face.

"Clear," the lead guard called out again. "Close the door."

The door slid closed with a solid clang. Apparently at least one more guard was watching and listening from some control booth.

The lead guard stood with his back to Ryland and Bree, giving more orders as the other three fastened Gerloff's chains to a massive steel loop in the tabletop. Once that was done, they attached his ankle chains to another thick loop on the floor underneath the table.

The three of them stepped back, behind Gerloff. "Prisoner secure, sir," one of them called out.

The lead guard circled the table, tugging on the chains. He leaned underneath it, tugging on those too before backing up. Apparently satisfied, he stepped back. The other guards backed away from the table too, spreading out around the room, all facing the prisoner.

The head guard finally turned toward Ryland and Bree. "You may not approach the prisoner. You're to sit in your chairs and remain there until the prisoner has been removed from the room. You have one hour, not a minute more. Questions?"

"Are you all staying for the interview?" Bree asked.

"Yes, ma'am. For your security."

Ryland motioned toward the table, and Gerloff, whose dark eyes were locked on him and Bree. "Do you secure every prisoner here the way you've secured Mr. Gerloff?"

"I can't discuss security protocol, sir. Please consider prisoner Gerloff to be exceptionally dangerous. Is that clear?"

"Clear. Thank you."

The guard waited until they'd taken their seats. Then he moved to stand about six feet behind the prisoner.

"Fifty-nine minutes," he called out.

"O…kay," Bree said. "Mr. Gerloff, thank you for agreeing to meet with us. This is Ryland Beck, former special agent with the TBI, currently an investigator with UB. I'm Detective Clark from Monroe County, and we—"

"I didn't agree to meet with anyone, lady. I agreed to see who wanted to talk to me, and then I'll make up my mind whether I'm going to answer any questions." Gerloff's gritty voice filled the room, its deep tone seeming to echo off the walls. He raked a glance across Bree, and then, as if dismissing her outright, focused on Ryland. "What's UB, TBI guy?"

Bree pursed her lips but remained silent.

Ryland started to lean forward in his chair, but the quick shake of the lead guard's head had him sitting straight. In all his years in law enforcement, he'd never once seen security this tight. It was bizarre, to say the least. But he wasn't going to question it. They obviously knew far more about their prisoner than he or Bree did. Something he'd remedy as soon as they were out of here. He was now extremely curious about Gerloff's background, especially since becoming a prisoner at this facility.

"UB stands for Unfinished Business. That's cop slang for a cold case. We're a civilian company that partners with law enforcement to try to solve cases that don't seem to have any leads."

"Unfinished Business," he mumbled, as if testing the syllables on his tongue. "I like that. Cold cases, huh? If you're here to ask me about some of those, trying to pin something on me, then we're done. I ain't talkin'." He yanked his arms, rattling the chains against the table.

The lead guard started forward, as if to end the interview.

"Wait," Ryland called out. "Please. We're not here to pin anything on you, sir. We're hoping you can help us with a current case involving Prosecutor Palmer of Monroe County, the county where you were arrested for your road rage…incident."

"Hold up," Gerloff said, raising a hand to signal the guard.

The guard stopped, his right hand poised on his baton as he waited.

"Palmer, huh?" Gerloff asked.

"Yes," Ryland confirmed. The light of interest in Gerloff's dark eyes told Ryland he'd stumbled onto the key that might get him to talk, so he went with it. "He's been arrested for murder."

Gerloff chuckled, his mouth curving in a chilling grin, gold flashing on the few teeth he still had. He glanced over his shoulder at the lead guard. "Cool your jets, Morris. I ain't talking to the female. But me and this UB fella have some things to discuss."

Bree stiffened beside Ryland. He wanted to reassure her, but he didn't want to do anything to change Gerloff's mind about the meeting, so he sat and waited.

The guard's face reddened slightly at the casual use of his name, but he stepped back, remaining several feet behind the prisoner.

"Palmer," Gerloff spat out. "Now there's a guy who deserves every bad thing that could possibly happen to him. Just look at me. I don't even have a record. Or, I didn't, until that guy cut me off on the highway." He shrugged, chains rattling. "Stuff happens, you know? But Palmer goes for the maximum penalty, convinces the judge I'm a 'danger to society.'" He held his fingers up, making air quotes, as he spoke. The chains rattled and clomped when he rested his arms on the table again. "Not surprised he snapped and killed somebody. The guy's not right in the head, you know. Who'd he kill?"

"We don't know that he killed anyone. He's been arrested, but the case against him is far from solid."

He frowned. "Why not? Aren't there witnesses who saw him? Who can swear he was there, where the bodies were found? I'll bet his car was seen in the area. Am I right?"

Ryland drew a slow, deep breath, careful to keep his expression blank. He hadn't said there was more than one murder, but Gerloff said *bodies*, plural. It sounded as if he knew about the murders. Was that because he'd seen news coverage? Or because he had insider knowledge? And him mentioning a car had Ryland especially suspicious, although that too may have been mentioned on the news.

"There are witnesses, yes," Ryland told him.

"I'm one of them. I saw him on a mountain road a short distance from where Detective Clark and I discovered one of the bodies."

His gaze flicked to Bree, then back to Ryland. "Discovered? How? What made you look for it? Was it hard to find?"

"Detective Clark and I went into the woods to find the man I believed was Prosecutor Palmer. She saw some things that made her suspicious, and is the one who actually found the grave."

He frowned and finally gave Bree his full attention. "What was suspicious?"

She looked at Ryland. "Should I tell him?"

Gerloff pounded his fist on the table. "What was suspicious?"

"The prisoner will keep his hands down and not hit the table," the lead guard said.

"Shove it, Morris. Tell me what was suspicious or this little visit is over."

Guard Morris turned a light shade of red again, but remained silent.

Ryland nodded, letting Bree know he felt it was okay to share the information. It seemed important to Gerloff. And Ryland wanted him to keep talking.

"There were gouges on the trees, one in each corner of the glade, marking off the points of a compass, north, south, east, west.

It made me think there might be a body buried in the middle."

He pointed to Ryland. "You answer this time. What do you mean, buried?"

Red alarm bells were going off inside Ryland's mind. Gerloff seemed surprised the body was buried. Why would he be surprised? Unless he knew the body wasn't supposed to be buried? Why would he know that? And why would he care? Unless… He looked at Bree and could tell by her expression that the same red flags were going off for her as well.

She cleared her throat, getting the lead guard's attention. "Sir, I need access to my phone. They made me lock it up with my purse and keys outside."

He frowned. "That's against protocol. You don't get your personal belongings back until you're outside of the prisoner area."

"It's really important. I just need to look up something on the internet. Please?"

"That door doesn't open during the interview. However, I can get another guard to look up what you need. Will that work?"

"Yes. Thank you."

He radioed for another guard. A moment later, the guard appeared in the hallway. He motioned to Bree and she hurried over, telling him what she needed.

Ryland continued the discussion with Gerloff, deciding to bluff and see what happened.

"Yep. We've got a copycat killer running around, trying to pass off his kills as if he was the Smoky Mountain Slayer. But he keeps screwing up, doing things wrong that make it obvious he's not the Slayer. Like burying his bodies instead of leaving them out in the open the way the Slayer did."

Gerloff stared at him, his eyes narrowing. "Is that right? He buries each one, does he? How many?"

"Two so far. But we intend to stop him before he kills again."

"You already have. Palmer's been arrested. I mean, that's what you said."

"Oh, we know that's not going to hold. The copycat has made some big mistakes. We're on his trail. Or, I should say, the police are. Detective Clark and I are following up with anyone who might have a grudge against Palmer, who might be working with the copycat on the outside to try to frame Palmer. That's why we wanted to talk to you, since you're one of the people Palmer told us might have a grudge against him. Your name was on the list he gave us of people who might be trying to frame him."

His face reddened. "Thought you weren't here to pin something on me."

Ryland shrugged.

Gerloff's face got even redder. But he was obviously wavering between cutting the interview short and satisfying his curiosity. Finally, he said, "Who else is on the list?"

Ryland barely managed not to grin. Gerloff's curiosity had won out. He told Gerloff the first name.

"Never heard of him. Keep going."

Ryland gave him another name. Gerloff made a comment that the guy was an idiot who couldn't tell his left shoe from his right.

"Nancy Compadre."

"A woman? Are you kidding me? Keep going."

Bree's back stiffened over by the bars. She was obviously listening to Gerloff, even as she continued to speak to the guard who was radioing to someone else what she wanted.

"Let's see. Dan Smith."

"The office killer?"

"He shot his boss and three other people, yes. He's at this same prison."

"Well, I ain't ever seen him here. Who else?"

"Liam Kline."

Gerloff stared at him a long moment. "Who else?"

Bingo.

Kline was the only one he hadn't said anything about. There was a connection there.

"Have you ever met Kline?"

"Nope. Never heard of him."

Bree turned around and jogged to her seat beside Ryland. She gave him a subtle nod, before facing Gerloff. "You're lying, Mr. Gerloff. Liam Kline was your cell mate. I just confirmed it. He was your cell mate from day one until he was released a year ago. Is he the one who's framing Prosecutor Palmer? Did you put him up to that? So you can get your revenge?"

He stared at her, his eyes darkening with anger, so dark they appeared black. Then he raised his arms, chains rattling, and held them out in front of him like claws, squeezing them in the universal sign of someone choking someone.

Ryland jumped to his feet. "We're done."

Morris ordered him to sit, but Ryland ignored him. He grabbed Bree's arm and hurried her to the door. "Let us out. Now."

Ten minutes later, they were sitting in the parking lot in his Rover.

He gently clasped her shoulder. "Are you okay?"

She gave him a grateful smile. "Thank you for getting us out of there. I've never felt so uncomfortable in my life."

"Well, I sure as hell wasn't going to sit and let him make threats. You said he and Kline were cell mates. What else did you find out?"

"It's more like what did your team find out. I texted Trent and asked him to give me everything he could find on Gerloff. One of the very first things he found out was that he was Kline's cell mate. As soon as I saw Kline's name, I knew we were on to something. Here, let me try to summarize what Trent sent."

She pulled up the email on her phone as Ryland headed out of the parking lot toward Gatlinburg. "Let's see, okay. We already know from Mrs. Kline that Liam was brutally attacked the first day he was in prison. I got the impression she thought it was his cell mate. But it wasn't. Some of the other prisoners ganged up on him in the prison yard. They got a huge group of inmates to crowd around, blocking the camera views. No one would admit to seeing what happened. No one was brought up on charges. Then, once Liam recovered, he was placed—not in solitary, as he should have been—but right back in the general population, with Gerloff as his cell mate. Apparently, Gerloff killed his previous cell mate, before Kline."

He glanced at her, stunned. "Sounds like someone wanted Kline dead."

"The warden thought so too. There was an

investigation, and five guards were fired. But when the warden was going to move Kline to solitary for his own protection, he refused, saying he wanted to stay with Gerloff."

Ryland shook his head, steering around a slow-moving car. "Why would he do that? Doesn't make sense."

"In hindsight, it does. No one touched Kline again after the attack. He never had to be locked up in solitary for protection either. And there were some mysterious deaths after that, five prisoners killed in various ways. Low-key. Quiet. No witnesses. No one brought up on charges. But get this. All five were in the prison yard the day that Kline was attacked."

Ryland nodded. "Okay, now it makes sense. For some reason, Gerloff takes a liking to Kline and offers his protection. He's got some kind of reputation in the prison. Other guys are scared of him. He takes out the ones who hurt Kline, and makes it known that if anyone else touches him, they'll be killed too. The only question is, what did Gerloff promise in return?"

"If you're thinking something sexual, I don't think so. Gerloff is completely homophobic. He's attacked guys if they just looked at him wrong."

"Gerloff hates Palmer. That was obvious back there."

"So does Kline. Maybe that's what drew them to each other, what they both had in common," she said.

"Where does that leave us? Kline was a decent guy before prison. Loses everything he cares about, including his looks. Then shares a cell with a scary, evil guy for three years, probably egging each other on over their mutual hatred of Palmer. Is that enough to turn Kline into a killer? Is he the guy I saw on the road, with a disguise that could fool a Hollywood makeup artist?"

"Are we completely giving up on the theory that Palmer did it? That he planned everything out to take suspicion off him?" she asked.

He blew out a deep breath. "It just feels too far out there to think he'd do that. I suppose it's possible. But I'm not putting my money on it."

"Me either. It's the whole KISS principle."

"Keep it simple, stupid?"

She laughed. "Exactly. Or Occam's razor, if we want to keep it a little more professional. The simplest explanation is usually the right explanation. Something along those lines. Although there's really nothing simple about any of our theories."

He chuckled. "Definitely not."

"Can you handle me making a theoretical leap here? I don't want to offend your investigator sensibilities by suggesting a theory without the facts to back it up yet."

He rolled his eyes. "I think I can handle it. Heck, I've been proposing wild theories all day. Go for it."

"In that case, I'm going to say the obvious and simplest answer seems to be that, yes, Kline is the copycat. He picked a case he knew Palmer was involved with and used it to try to frame him. He pretended to be Palmer and killed two people. The first one is someone Palmer knew was guilty, but got off on a technicality. I'll bet when we get the ID on the latest victim, they'll be in that same category—someone Palmer prosecuted but got off, someone guilty. The setup is that Palmer felt justified in killing them because they were guilty. And he resented they'd damaged his nearly perfect prosecutorial track record."

"And Kline? What does he get out of this? The satisfaction that Palmer goes to prison?" He blinked and glanced at her. She looked just as stunned as he felt.

"Ryland—"

"Give me a second." He pulled to the shoulder and put the Rover in Park before turning to face her. "Do I say it? Or you?"

She smiled. "It's your turn."

"Gerloff and Kline both hate Palmer and

want him to pay for putting them in prison. They fantasize together for years about how they'd destroy Palmer if either of them ever get out. Then Kline's appeal is successful. But even people who are exonerated are rarely released the day the judge rules on the case. Paperwork has to be filed, plans made. He could have spent another day, a week, maybe even a month in prison if things went slowly. Knowing he was going to be set free, he makes a plan with Gerloff to get even with Palmer. Maybe in the beginning it was about Kline filing the civil suit alleging prosecutorial misconduct. But Palmer never had to publicly admit to any misconduct, and he didn't lose his job. Maybe Plan B all along was to frame him. Gerloff advises him on how to kill. He's obviously killed far more people than the one road rage victim. And you can tell he's a sociopath just by looking at him. I'll bet that road rage incident was one of many murders even before Gerloff went to prison."

"More guesses, without facts, Ryland?" she teased.

"You've ruined me. What can I say?"

"I think you were going to say what we've both figured out, the Plan B goal in all of this."

He nodded. "Prison has been the ultimate punishment for Gerloff and Kline, hell on earth.

They want Palmer to experience that kind of hell. Kline is framing Palmer so he'll go to prison. And by ensuring he's framed for heinous crimes, he'll be sent to maximum security, the same prison as Gerloff. That's the payback to Gerloff for saving Kline's life. Palmer suffers the indignity of going to prison. And Gerloff gets to do whatever he wants to Palmer."

Chapter Twenty

Ryland and Bree sat at the small desk in the two-bedroom hotel suite he'd gotten them so they could share his laptop for the impromptu meeting with the UB team. They'd just finished updating the team on everything that had happened. Their law enforcement liaison, Rowan, was now calling Sheriff Peterson and Chief Russo to provide them with updates. No doubt one of them would issue a BOLO soon so that law enforcement in the area would be on the lookout for Kline, using the picture that Faith had managed to get from the prison while Bree and Ryland gave their update. It was the picture the prison took the day he was being released, and Kline's face was just as ravaged as his ex-wife had described. Seeing him like that had cemented Ryland's belief that Kline really could be their guy, that a once good man could turn bad when everything he cared about had been taken from him.

Brice and Asher gave their updates about the Rogers case, including that she'd been visiting Gatlinburg during the time she was killed. It certainly seemed like a glaring coincidence that Palmer was also in Gatlinburg at the same time.

Palmer's alibis for the times of both recent murders couldn't be corroborated. He'd taken vacation days both times.

"Did Gatlinburg PD agree to let our lab run the Amido Black test to look for fingerprints on Rogers's skin?" Ryland asked.

Lance motioned to get everyone's attention. "I'll take that one. The police here have been extremely cooperative and gave our lab techs full access. Our people performed the test at the morgue, rather than bring the body to UB, per the medical examiner's request. Unfortunately, no fingerprints were found. It's possible the killer wore gloves, but given the decayed state of the body and small of amount of skin available for testing, it may just be that any fingerprints are long gone."

"It was worth a shot," Ryland said. "Any luck finding potential suspects who look like Palmer and have been seen in the area?"

"I've got that one," Faith said. "I hit the pavement downtown with Palmer's picture. Went to all the antique stores and restaurants. Talked to a gazillion people, and quite a few remembered seeing him downtown. But there's no way to know if it was Prosecutor Palmer or someone disguised to look like him. The timing lined up with what Palmer said, so it's possible he was in town antiquing at the time he said he was. Kind of hard to prove either way. I was hoping to find witnesses who think they saw Palmer when he wasn't supposedly in Gatlinburg, but that was a bust."

Bree sighed heavily. "Sounds like you guys and gals are working hard, but we've got a long way to go to get enough facts to move forward."

"We've only been at this a handful of days," Ryland said. "Considering what we started with, I think we're on track. We'll get it done. Don't worry."

"Oh, I don't doubt it at all. It's just been incredibly stressful and I was hoping for a miracle, I suppose, like some real forensic evidence that could act as a flashing neon sign for us."

"Even with a lab on site, forensics can take a bit of time. And I gave Ivy and Callum a huge list of things to work on, maybe too huge. Did either of you get anywhere with looking into the cold case aspect of all this?"

Ivy motioned at Callum, who was with her at UB headquarters in a conference room for the meeting. "You've talked to the families of two of the Slayer victims so far, right?"

"Right. Just finished up with Sanford, and I spoke to the Cardenas relatives earlier this morning. Tomorrow I've got Morrison and Wilcox lined up. The Morton family is out of the country on vacation. I'm working through the time zone differences with them for a conference call, possibly later tonight. Or, rather, really early tomorrow morning, like around two. I was able to revisit the body dump sites of all five victims, but nothing struck me that wasn't already covered in the original reports. As to Sanford and Cardenas, I've got a lot of information on their friends, families, where they liked to shop, eat, things like that. And I'm building a timeline of their last days. No overlap between them, though, not that I've found so far. Oh, and no ties to Palmer that I've been able to find."

Ivy chimed in. "I'm going to help him with all that eventually. For now, I've been working on a lot of the other things you wanted, like getting the Slayer cases uploaded to social media sites and websites devoted to bringing public awareness to cold cases. I've submitted requests to obtain cell phone records from their respective carriers. Oh, and when Callum visited each of the dump sites, he got me some great pictures and measurements of the marks the killer made in the trees. I took pictures and measurements at the site up here, where Rogers was found. All of it's been sent to a tool mark analysis expert to see if the same tools were used for all the murder scenes."

"That's great," Ryland said. "You've got the ball rolling on a lot of analysis. That should really help when we start getting the results back."

"Thanks, but I'm not done. Let's see, what else…" She swiped through several screens of notes on her computer tablet. "Okay, here we go. I've hired a geographical profiling expert to compare all the cases. He's new to us, but Trent recommended him from a case he worked before coming to UB. And I got in touch with the original special agent who did the profile for Bree's office when she was investigating the Slayer. I know we want a different profiler this time, but I also didn't want to insult the original agent and cause UB any problems in the future. So I very nicely and carefully explained that we were looking for fresh eyes on this and had a new case to consider as well, the Rogers case. And of course the newest one that just happened, but I don't have solid information on that one just yet. It went pretty well. He gave me another contact, and that guy has a lot more experience. I'm hoping for a profile in the next few days. Well, two profiles, actually, as you requested. One without the Rogers case and one with." She swiped through her notes, then sat back. "I've got a lot more to look into but that's it so far."

Bree laughed. "Ivy, I think you got more done in a few days than I'd get done in a week. I'm super impressed with you, with all of you. Thank you so much for your hard work."

"Of course," Ivy said, smiling. "Happy to help."

"Thanks Ivy," Ryland added. "I agree, everyone's done a tremendous amount of work. I think the elephant in the room that no one has mentioned yet, though, is DNA. I was hoping the evidence from the Slayer cases would be re-tested, and that Gatlinburg PD might allow our lab to test for DNA on the Rogers murder. Has anyone had any traction with that?"

Trent, who'd been typing on his computer for most of the call, waved at the camera. "I can speak to that."

Ryland sighed heavily. "Honestly, I think your report on guardrails can wait."

Several of the investigators laughed.

Trent made a wounded look. "I'm shocked you don't find my construction bidding process to make travel safer for all of us riveting. But I'll forgo that report today. You were asking about DNA. I'm your man. Everyone else was socked with work, so I volunteered to work with Rowan to get the evidence to the lab, and I checked in with Chief Russo about the Rogers case. The Rogers case is still being looked into by the medical examiner, and they're not ready to send samples over. But they will. As for the rest, I literally just got a report in my email on that. Hold on to your seats, folks." He cracked his knuckles like a major league pitcher getting ready to throw a fast ball.

"Hold it," Ryland said. "Does this mean you didn't look into what happened with Bree's SUV being forced over a cliff?"

"I hate to save him from a thrashing," Brice spoke up. "But I took point on that, and there really isn't a lot that he could do that I'm not doing. I'm actively working with Gatlinburg PD but don't have anything yet."

"Hey, hey, hey," Trent said. "Ivy reached out to me for help. This is legit."

Ryland arched a brow. "Ivy?"

She held her hands out in a helpless gesture. "You did tell Callum and me that if we ended up needing help to ask someone else on the team. I asked Trent."

Ryland groaned.

Ivy grinned.

"Before you guys duke it out," Faith spoke up, "I forgot to tell you as part of my report that I called the Monroe County medical examiner's office to check on the latest murder victim. Sheriff Peterson has a standing order for everyone to share information with UB, so that really helped. The victim who was killed late last night, or early this morning, however you look at it, was Stephanie Zimmer."

"I should have guessed," Bree said.

"You knew her too?" Ryland asked.

"Knew *of* her. Another one of those rare cases Palmer lost. And like Rogers, she was obviously guilty. She poisoned her husband. A search warrant issue had key evidence in the case thrown out. There wasn't enough evidence after that to get a conviction, so she walked."

"Bree," Trent said, "I really like you, but you're on my time right now. I've got important stuff to say."

She laughed at his teasing. "My apologies. Go ahead."

"Hold that thought." This time it was Callum who spoke up. "Ryland, that side research into Palmer's prosecution win percentage is shaping up. There's definitely something going on there, and it's not just what happened to Liam Kline. I should have the final report from the private investigator in Monroe County by the end of this week."

"Thanks, Callum."

"Enough. I'm not kidding." Trent sounded exasperated. "I just got some information and, trust me, you really want to hear this."

Ryland glanced at Bree before looking back at the computer. "All right. What do you have?"

Trent leaned toward the camera. "This literally just came through. Our lab was able to find DNA on two of the Slayer's old cases. Thanks to the Monroe County Sheriff's Office, the evidence was perfectly preserved, and the DNA wasn't degraded. Ladies and gentlemen, we have the DNA profile of the Smoky Mountain Slayer."

Bree pumped her fist in the air. "Yes! All we have to do is put it into CODIS and hope there's a hit—"

"That would take days, maybe longer. I went on a hunch, based on what you and Ryland have been telling us. I specifically asked for a comparison with a specific person. I was right. We have a match."

Bree stared at the screen in shock. "Are you telling us you know the identity of the Smoky Mountain Slayer?"

He smiled in triumph. "I certainly do. His name, ladies and gentlemen, is Silas Gerloff."

Chapter Twenty-One

Nearly a week later, Bree was cursing beneath her breath and trying, without any luck, to get comfortable in a hard plastic chair at the Monroe County Sheriff's Office.

Ryland chuckled beside her. "You're not big on waiting, are you?"

She shifted again. "These chairs are awful. I can't believe my boss is making us sit in the public waiting area until he's ready to meet with us."

"Maybe it's his way of reminding you that you're officially on leave, essentially a civilian. I'm sure he's not happy that you were involved in the investigation with me."

"I'm not on leave anymore. My week has been up for several days."

"I seem to remember a requirement about meeting with a doctor before you came back."

"Pfft. I'm sure he's not going to enforce that. It's silly. I'm obviously fine. Besides, we solved the Slayer case for him." She motioned toward the TV on the opposite wall, with a banner scrolling across the bottom. "It's all over the news. The way you and Grayson spun things, it gives most of the credit to the Monroe County Sheriff's Office. Peterson should be thrilled about that, and that Gerloff has been charged. Plus, it's only a matter of time before they catch Kline. Thanks to your lab finding DNA at the two most recent murder sites, and comparing it to the profile on record with the Tennessee violent offender database, we have a match. Kline is the copycat."

She looked up at him. "The part that sucks is that Palmer's in the clear and has been released. I would have preferred he experience the hospitality of the county jail a little longer. That file you've got with you proves everything Kline was trying to prove, that Palmer cared more about his winning percentage than whether someone was innocent."

He tapped the folder on his lap. "Don't worry about Palmer. When Peterson sees this, his days as lead prosecutor are numbered. He'll probably be disbarred and likely come up on charges."

She motioned toward the news report on the TV. "I just wish we could tell that to the media. It would be nice to get all the fawning over Palmer off the news and tell people what he's really like, that he doesn't deserve their sympathy. He may have been Gerloff's and Kline's victim as far as setting him up, but he did far worse to so many people."

He put his hand on top of hers where it rested on her chair. "What's really bothering you? Everything's working out. Peterson may yell a little, or a lot, to make sure you know he's still the boss. But he's not going to fire you. After everything you've done to close the Slayer case, as well as the copycat case, he wouldn't dare. So what's the real problem?"

She looked at his hand on top of hers and had to blink back unexpected tears. The problem was that she didn't want to ever let go. She'd finally found what she really wanted—him—and now they were about to go their separate ways. Him to Gatlinburg, her to her house ten minutes away. There weren't any more excuses for her to stay at his house.

And there wasn't any point in trying to explore this…whatever it was between them. A long-distance relationship wasn't an option when neither of them wanted to give up their respective careers. And driving two hours to work each day and two hours home? That would get old fast, wearing both of them down.

"Bree? What's wrong?"

Dare she tell him? She looked up into his

handsome face, those gorgeous green eyes riveted on her as if the only thing in the world that mattered right now was finding out what was bothering her. He cared about her. No doubt. But did he care as much as she hoped?

She had to take a chance. If she didn't, she'd regret it for the rest of her life. There had to be a way to overcome the distance between them, literally, the two-hour commute. She didn't have a clue what the solution might be. But at least if she told him how much she cared about him, how desperately she wanted to explore a relationship with him that didn't involve bad guys and flying off cliffs, he'd know how she felt. And then he could let her know if he felt the same. Even rejection, as much as it would devastate her, was better than not knowing.

She drew a steadying breath, then slowly turned her hand palm-up, threading her fingers with his.

His brows rose, and his gaze shot to their joined hands. His Adam's apple bobbed in his throat. "Bree? Is there something you want to tell me?"

"Yes. There is. I—"

"Detective Clark, Mr. Beck, the sheriff will see you now," a voice called out.

Bree groaned at the sight of Peterson's ad-

ministrative assistant in the waiting room doorway, motioning for them to follow her.

Ryland squeezed her hand, then stood, pulling her with him.

"I don't want to go," she complained.

He laughed. "You can't put off talking to
him forever. It's the only way to get reinstated
at your job. Besides…" He held up the folder.
"Justice awaits."

SHERIFF PETERSON GLANCED up from his desk
as Ryland and Bree walked into his office. If
Bree didn't know him better, the thunderous
frown on his face would have scared her right
back to the waiting room. But he was all bark,
very little bite, as long as he respected you and
trusted you. And she'd never done anything to
make him not trust her. Well, except for not following his orders about not working the case.
And she hadn't gone to the therapist. She bit
her lip. Maybe she should be worried after all.

"Close the door," he ordered, his voice gruff.

Ryland closed it, then shook hands with him
before taking a seat across from Bree in front
of his desk.

"Good to see you again, Sheriff," Ryland
said. "Under much better circumstances than
when UB discussed taking on the Slayer cold
case six or seven weeks ago."

Since her boss was glaring at her until Ryland started talking, she gave Ryland a grateful look for drawing his attention.

"Yeah, well," Peterson said to Ryland. "Things turned out much better than I ever anticipated. We're building a strong case against Gerloff for the Slayer killings. The DNA evidence your company was able to get seals the deal. It's a huge relief bringing this to a resolution and getting justice for the victims and their families."

"Unfinished Business isn't done yet. Aside from Adam Trent working with your detective team, I'm happy to bring more investigators here if you need them. In Gatlinburg, two of them—Ivy Shaw and Callum Wright—are supporting what Trent's working on here, chasing down loose ends, hunting for more evidence. We'll follow your lead at this point and transition to a background role. We won't quit until you've got everything you need for the prosecution of Gerloff, and Kline as well, once he's located."

"Much appreciated. I know Detective Mills has been grateful for the help from that Trent fellow. As for the Rogers and Zimmer murders, your work on that has helped us avoid those becoming cold cases too. Without your lab's touch-DNA tests proving Kline was at both crime scenes, I don't know that we could have gotten him on those. He really knew what he was doing, wearing gloves and keeping the bodies so pristine and devoid of forensic evidence. I hear the DNA you found was on some of the leaves and debris in both locations that you got after performing a follow-up CSI collection at both sites. And that the DNA you collected is most likely from sweat that dripped off Kline's forehead as he dumped the bodies. It's amazing you were able to key in on that." He frowned. "Of course now it's a matter of finding him. Kind of hard to find a guy when the only picture we've got is over a year old. And we don't know if he's still using his Palmer disguise."

Bree sat forward in her chair. "At least the public has been alerted that if they see someone they believe is Palmer, that they should be careful, and of course look for the telltale signs of a mask. Up close, it should be easy to tell the difference. Not that we want anyone that close to him."

He slowly turned to face her, his expression hardening. "What part of me ordering you not to participate in the investigations and to get some rest did you not understand?"

She blinked. "I, ah, I did get some rest. Sort of. And—"

"From what I hear, you've been poking that

nose of yours into all things Slayer-related from the moment Mr. Beck rescued you from that cliff. Why are you even here? You should be home right now."

"My week is long up. I even went several days past that. Now I'm back, ready to help Mills and the rest of the team wrap up the loose ends on the investigations."

"Oh, well, in that case. Just hand me the doctor's note and I'll let you be on your way." He held out his hand and arched a brow in challenge.

"You, ah, weren't really serious about making me see a shrink, were you?"

He crossed his forearms on his desk. "You don't seriously want us to lose a case, and let a bad guy go free because you were too selfish to follow protocol and get cleared to return to duty, do you? I warned you about what defense attorneys would do if you aren't cleared."

She crossed her arms. "You're not playing fair."

He rolled his eyes. "Bree, I appreciate everything you, Mr. Beck and UB did. More than you can possibly imagine. But I don't make these rules just to hear myself talk. It's important. PTSD is nothing to joke about. Call the doctor. Make an appointment. Until then, you're still on leave."

She grumbled beneath her breath.

"What was that? Were you thanking me for not firing you for insubordination? Is that what you were saying?"

She forced a smile. "Of course. Yes, I was thanking you. Sir."

"You're welcome. Now, if there's nothing else—"

"Actually," she said, "there is one more thing. It's about Palmer. I heard he's been released. Is he back at the office? Is he in today?"

"He's been released, but unlike you, he has enough sense to follow protocol. He's on administrative leave and has already been seeing the therapist over the stress of everything that's gone on."

"Leave it to Palmer to make me look bad."

"Don't blame Palmer for your actions. Why are you asking about him anyway?"

She was still stinging from his rebuke, but supposed she deserved it. "We want to interview him."

He straightened. "Interview him? About what? The man was framed for murder. What do you want to talk to him about?"

She motioned to Ryland. "You want to answer that one?"

He tossed the folder on top of the desk. "When we believed that Palmer might be a killer, UB dug into every facet of his life. One of the items that came under scrutiny was his incredible winning percentage as a prosecutor. I've personally never heard of any prosecutor with a percentage that high. And there's a reason for that. It's not legit." He motioned toward the folder. "What you'll find in there is evidence of gross prosecutorial misconduct on many of his cases. Bree and I wanted to ask Palmer some questions about all that. But since you're making her continue her administrative leave, I'm happy to turn the information over to you to do with as you see fit. And I'll be glad to drive Bree home."

She frowned at him, but when she would have complained, Peterson flipped open the folder.

"Gross prosecutorial misconduct, huh? Can I assume you mean he withheld information from the defense that could have been exculpatory, like what happened in the Kline case? He purposely allowed defendants to go to prison, even though he had evidence that might exonerate them?"

"Yes sir. Exactly that. There's a pattern, too much of a pattern to be an accident, as was argued in Kline's civil case."

He sat back. "I should have argued harder with the mayor after that civil suit. I told him he should fire Palmer. But the mayor wanted to give him another chance, in case it really was an accident."

Bree leaned forward again. "You really did that? Argued to fire him?"

"You and Mr. Beck aren't the only ones to be suspicious of that winning percentage. I imagine some of the cases I've questioned over the years are in this folder. But getting the mayor to let us look into it is a whole other matter." He tapped the folder. "Thank you, Mr. Beck. I don't think the mayor can ignore this now. Not after Kline went on a killing spree because of Palmer's actions. And not with the evidence you've got in here. Palmer's days around here are numbered."

Peterson stood. "If that's all, I've got another meeting to get to. And you, *Detective* Clark, need to go home. I'll set up an appointment for you at nine tomorrow to see the doctor. If she gives you the all clear, consider yourself reinstated."

"Oh, thank you, sir. I really appreciate it."

"Go on. Before I change my mind." He softened his order with a smile.

Bree smiled back, and headed out of his office with Ryland.

Chapter Twenty-Two

"Here we are again," Bree said, as Ryland pulled his Rover up to her house. "Feels like forever since I've been home." She waved through the windshield at her neighbor, Mrs. Riley, who was in her front yard, weeding.

"It's been one of the longest toughest stretches in my life too. But it hasn't all been bad. Some of it has been pretty damn good."

She blinked. "It has?"

He smiled, that slow sexy smile that made her stomach jump. "Oh, yeah. *Really* good."

She cleared her throat. "Would you like to come inside with me? Maybe we can talk about the really good part?"

He leaned over and pressed an achingly sweet kiss against her lips. But it was over far too soon. "Bree, I'd love to come in and…talk. I really would. But I have an errand to run first. It's important, and I'm not sure how long it will take. An hour, maybe longer, maybe not. As soon as I can, I'll come back. Okay?"

An errand. She sighed. "Okay. If it takes a while, don't worry about the time. I'll wait. I mean, I'll be here. I'm not going anywhere." Inwardly she cringed at how desperate and needy she sounded.

She opened the Rover's door, but before she could hop out, he asked, "Bree? You really love it here, right? Madisonville? Your job at the sheriff's office?"

"Well, yeah. I do." She searched his gaze, hoping. "Why do you ask?"

"No reason. Just thinking. Your neighbor seems really nice. Mrs. Riley, right? The one who helped you get back into your house after, well—"

"My purse and keys ended up at the bottom of the mountain?" She smiled. "Yes. She's a nice lady. Ryland—"

"I need to get going."

Her smile faded. "Right. Your errand."

"See you later," he said as she got out of the truck. "And, Bree? Be careful. Don't open your door to anyone, especially if you don't know them, or they look like Palmer. I'm telling you, that mask Kline has is incredibly lifelike."

She patted her jacket pocket. "I'm carrying.

Don't worry. And I'm not opening the door for anyone but you."

Again, desperate-sounding. But his warm smile had her whole body tingling. Her pride came to her rescue, keeping her from begging him to skip his errand. As nonchalantly as she could, she waved goodbye and headed into her house.

She closed the door and flipped the dead bolt.

The unmistakable sound of a shotgun being pumped had her freezing.

"Hello there, Bree," a raspy voice called out from behind her.

Very slowly, she turned around. She blinked in shock to see Prosecutor Palmer standing in her foyer, pointing a shotgun at her chest. She'd have sworn on the stack of Bibles Ryland had once mentioned that the man standing four feet away was the real Palmer. But the voice was different, telling her this was fake-Palmer.

"Amazing, isn't it?" He turned his face left and right. "Cost a fortune in plastic surgery to get it just right."

"Plastic surgery?"

"I tried a mask at first, but it was never as realistic as I needed it to be. And since my face was destroyed in prison," he spat out, "I needed a new one. The state wouldn't pay to fix my face, to make me look human again. But they paid in the end, after I sued them for everything they were worth. Oh, where are my manners? Allow me to formally introduce myself. Liam Kline, at your service."

She dove to the side, clawing for her pistol.

He dropped down on top of her, giving her wrist a vicious twist.

She cried out and dropped the gun. It skittered across the floor.

He leaned down, his body pressing on hers, his face twisting with rage. The eyes. The eyes were off. They were brown, like Palmer's. But there was nothing behind them, an empty pit of nothingness, as if he'd traded his soul to the devil.

"You and that Ryland guy ruined everything. I was excited at first when I heard the rumors around town that UB was re-opening the Slayer case. Nothing else I'd tried had worked to make Palmer pay, and I figured this was my chance, that I could frame him as the Smoky Mountain Slayer. So I killed Rogers and planned my next steps. All I had to do was make sure someone from UB saw me the day Palmer went to Gatlinburg, thought I was him, then found the body where I'd planted his wallet. Then I'd do whatever else I could to push, keep piling on more supposed evidence to make sure they believed Palmer was the bad guy."

"Like pushing my truck off a cliff? And trying to make it look like Palmer had done it?" She inched one of her hands back toward where she thought her pistol had fallen. But the way he was pressing against her, she couldn't turn her head to look for it.

"Exactly like that. It was kind of a spur-of-the-moment thing. But I was watching from the woods when you drove up to UB in that Monroe County Sheriff's SUV. It didn't take any inside knowledge to figure out you were bringing the evidence from the Slayer case. What better way to escalate things than to kill you and frame Palmer for it? Doesn't matter that you didn't die. As long as Palmer was blamed."

He narrowed his eyes. "But after finding that body, instead of accepting the clues I was leaving that pointed to Palmer as the killer, you and Ryland got too nosy for your own good. You talked to Gerloff and figured out his connection to me. Everything fell apart after that. Revenge was the only thing I had left to live for, and you took it from me. Now you're going to pay. *Both of you.*"

A burst of white-hot pain exploded in her skull as the butt of the shotgun slammed against the side of her head.

Chapter Twenty-Three

Ryland had proof that the entrepreneurial spirit was alive and well in Madisonville, or at least as far as Melanie Holland was concerned. She'd demanded an outrageous sum to sell Bree's painting to him. But he'd gladly paid, using his own money, not UB's, knowing how much it meant to Bree. With the painting safely stowed in the back of his Rover, he headed back to her house.

He was a block away when his phone buzzed with an incoming text message. With so much going on with the investigations right now, he didn't want to ignore it. He pulled to the curb to read the text. It was from Bree.

Ryland, I have a few more details to add to the investigation. Can you come to my house?

He stared at the text a long moment, then typed his reply.

ETA ten minutes. See you soon.

Three dots on the screen showed she was typing her reply.

Okay. See you in ten.

He quickly navigated to his favorite contacts and pressed a button.

The voice came through the phone on the first ring. "Hey, Ry, what's going—"

"Trent. Please tell me you're still at the sheriff's office."

"I'm still at the sheriff's office. Why? What's—"

"I just got a weird text from Bree. She asked me to come over to discuss the investigation."

"The investigation is over from her standpoint, isn't it?"

"Exactly. But the weird part is, she already knew I was coming back. And it wasn't to discuss the case."

"Ah. I see. So… I'm not sure I follow. What's the problem?"

"Has Kline been caught yet?"

"No. And I'd know, believe me. I'm sitting with Detective Mills right now. He'd be one of the first to hear about it."

"I don't think Bree sent that text. I think

Kline is at her house, right now, with her." He glanced at the time on the dash clock. "If I'm not at her house in a few minutes, Kline's going to kill her. We have to figure out a way to save her, now."

Ryland spoke fast, bouncing ideas off Trent while keeping a close eye on the time. He didn't want to risk going past that ten-minute ETA. He could have bluffed for an even longer amount of time, but he also didn't want her alone with Kline any longer than she had to be.

Six precious minutes had flown by since Bree's, or Kline's, text to him. After he hung up with Trent, he dialed another number in his contact list.

And prayed they would take his call.

Chapter Twenty-Four

Bree twisted her bound hands behind the back of the chair she was tied to, desperately trying to get free without allowing her body or the chair to move enough to alert Kline.

He paced in front of her like a caged tiger from one end of the family room to the other. The dining room chair he'd dragged into the middle of the room for her to sit on faced the front door, and she had no doubt as to why. When Ryland got here, the first thing he'd see was her, tied up, a gag in her mouth. From there, it would go one of two ways. When Ryland rushed in to save her, Kline would either fire a bullet into Ryland, or he'd fire one into her. Either way, one of them was going to experience the horror of seeing the other one die before Kline finished them off.

Regret was heavy on her mind as she thought about the things she wished she could change. Like that night at Ryland's home when she'd kissed him, then went into the bedroom alone. She'd been terrified by the depth of her emotions for a man she'd just met, and terrified at the prospect of losing her heart to him with all the obstacles in their way. Now, she might never have a chance to tell him how she really felt—that she was as in love with him as she could possibly be. Two weeks or two years, didn't matter. Ryland meant everything to her. And he'd never know it. Why, oh why hadn't she told him?

Of course, she knew why. They were both consumed with their careers, neither of them even considering giving up their jobs to move the two hours away to the other's town. And she'd known him for such a short amount of time, it was difficult to trust her feelings. Were her feelings real? Were they brought on by the trauma they'd shared after her truck went over the cliff? Or were they the foundation of forever, worth giving up a career and her hometown?

She loved him. But did he love her? The fear that he didn't, a very real fear given that neither of them had spoken about their feelings, was what held her back. What would probably still hold her back even now, even if she had a chance to tell him.

It didn't matter. None of that mattered right

now. What mattered was figuring out some way to save Ryland. There was no way she was getting out of this alive. But if she could do something to alert him, to warn him, maybe he would survive.

She worked and twisted at the rope around her wrists. How long had it been? She was running out of time. Ryland would be here soon.

Kline paced back and forth, back and forth, mumbling to himself. Suddenly, he stopped in front of a decorative mirror on the far wall, as if he'd been working up his courage and that was his goal all along. To get up the nerve to look at his reflection.

He stared at it a long moment, slowly turning his head this way and that. Then he roared with rage and slammed his face against the mirror. Bree let out a startled yelp behind her gag, jerking her head the other way as pieces of glass rained down on her.

"Don't turn away from me," he ordered, suddenly right in front of her, blood welling up from cuts on his face, his neck. "Look at me." His fingers curled like talons. "Do you have any idea what it's like to see the face of your enemy every time you catch your reflection? Do you?" He raked his nails down his cheeks, leaving bloody welts in their tracks. "Do you?"

She leaned as far back as the chair would

allow, shaking her head no. Her wrists throbbed, something hot and wet running down her fingers. Blood, probably. But she couldn't stop. She had to get free.

He slowly straightened, eyes narrowed, blood dripping. "You'd never know it, Bree. But I was a good-looking guy before your prosecutor railroaded me into prison. I had a family, a wife, sons, a career. Palmer took all of that away. Then I was forced to pretend I liked a man I despised, a monster, who whispered sickening details about the people he'd tortured and killed every night as I lay in my bunk, trying to sleep so I could escape the hell my life had become, if only for a few hours. But there was no escape. His tales followed me into my dreams, my nightmares. And even if he hadn't told me all that, everyone in the prison knew how sick and twisted he was. Anyone who crossed him got hurt. Even the guards were afraid of him." He grabbed her shoulders. "Are you listening to me? Do you know what you've done?" He slapped her, slamming her cheek against the back of the chair.

She cried out against the gag, her cheek throbbing with pain.

Then, as if a switch had flipped, the demented monster cocked his head, studying her as a bird might eye a worm, or a cat might eye a bird. But instead of pouncing, he slowly straightened. He used the edge of his shirt to wipe at the blood on his face, then cleared his throat and pulled a pistol out of his pocket.

Bree tensed, watching the pistol, his finger, as he stroked the trigger.

"I've never killed an innocent person before," he said. "Not that you police are innocent, but you get my meaning, right?" His tone was conversational, as if they were two friends discussing their plans for the coming weekend. "I only used the knowledge Gerloff gave me to kill bad people, dangerous people, monsters like him who should have been locked away, and who would have been if not for Palmer's incompetence."

He spit the name Palmer as if it was an epithet. His nostrils flared, and he began to pace again, his pistol clutched in his right hand.

She twisted again, ever so slightly. One of the loops around her wrist fell away! But not enough for her to free a hand. She picked at the rope, working at the next loop.

He stopped pacing a few feet from her and pulled out his phone to look at the screen.

Another loop fell away. Bree froze, hoping he couldn't tell there was some slack in the rope where it tied her waist to the chair.

He frowned and put away the phone. "He

should have been here by now." He raised his gun, aiming it at her head. "Looks like I don't get that grand finale I was going for."

"Kline! Freeze!"

He whirled around, firing shots down the hall where the voice had come from.

Bree screamed behind the gag and shoved her feet against the floor, using the momentum to propel herself and the chair against Kline's legs.

They both crashed to the floor, the chair hitting his shoulder.

Kline roared with rage and shoved the chair off him, throwing it, and Bree, against the coffee table. She landed on her side, the metallic taste of blood filling her mouth. She rocked the chair, ignoring the pain as she desperately tried to yank the loosened ropes free.

Kline slowly rose to his feet.

Bree looked past him, down the hall. Was that Ryland who'd tried to help her? Had he been shot? *Please, God, let him be okay. Let him live.*

Kline raised his pistol, his face mottled and red as he pointed it at her once again.

The front door crashed open, slamming against the wall with a loud bang.

Kline dove across Bree and whirled her chair around like a shield, crouching behind it with his gun thrust against her cheek. "Just in time, Beck. You get to see me kill sweet curvy Bree."

Beck? Bree twisted toward the door. Ryland stood in the opening, aiming his gun at Kline.

"Shoot her, and you won't get to talk to your wife." Ryland held up his phone, the screen facing them. "She's right here, Kline. She's on the phone. You can see her, talk to her. She wants to talk to you."

"Becky?" Kline's voice was filled with wonder and hope. "Is that really you?" He frowned. "I can't hear her. Turn up the volume."

"Move away from Bree. Come into the foyer so you can talk to Becky."

Kline shoved the gun harder against Bree's cheek. "Turn it up. Bring it closer so I can see her."

"It's as high as it goes. And I'm not going anywhere until you turn your gun away from Bree." Ryland looked down at the phone. "What's that. Mrs. Kline? You're going to hang up if he doesn't let Bree go?"

"No!" Kline lunged to his feet, but kept the gun jammed against Bree's temple. "Drop your gun. Do it!"

Ryland dropped his gun. "She's going to hang up, Kline. I had to beg her to talk to you, but she doesn't want to see this, to see what you've become. I convinced her there was still some good in you. But you're proving me wrong."

"Give me the phone!" Kline jumped over the chair.

A sound came from the hallway. Trent lurched into the opening, blood dripping from his wrist as he brought up his pistol.

Kline whirled toward him, firing.

Trent fell to the floor.

Bree screamed, but only a muffled sound came out behind her gag.

Ryland tossed the phone at Kline.

"Becky!" Kline jumped to catch the phone.

Ryland scrambled for his pistol where it had slammed against the wall when he'd dropped it.

Kline caught the phone, a twisted smile on his lips as he lifted it. He looked at the screen, then shouted with rage. Ryland lunged for his gun on the floor as Kline whirled his pistol toward him.

Bam! Bam! Bam!

Bree stared in horror as the gun fell from Ryland's hands. His chest heaved as his gaze met hers. Then Kline gurgled and dropped to the floor, his eyes rolling up in his head.

Ryland pushed himself to his feet, then went to Kline, kicking his gun away. He pressed his fingers against his neck, checking for a pulse.

He looked at Bree and shook his head. Then he ran to her and quickly untied her.

He pulled her onto his lap on the floor and yanked the gag off over her head. "Bree, how bad are you hurt?" His hands shook as he gently wiped blood from her mouth. "Bree?" he choked on her name.

"I'm... I'm okay," she whispered, her throat raw. "That psychopath slapped me and I bit my tongue."

Ryland's mouth twitched, then he grinned and chuckled. "You bit your tongue?"

"It's not funny! It hurts!"

He threw his head back and laughed, his shoulders shaking. But he quickly sobered and hugged her to his chest. "I thought I was too late. I heard the shots. I thought—"

"Trent! Ryland, he got shot. I think... I think Kline killed him."

Ryland kissed her, a quick warm kiss that she'd have reveled in at any other time. She tugged his hands down from her shoulders.

"Did you hear me? I think Trent's dead."

He didn't seem all that concerned as he turned slightly to look down the hall. "You dead, Trent?"

"Dead sore, that's what I am." He stumbled into the family room, clutching his bloody hand as he plopped onto the couch. "That jerk shot me four times. Knocked the wind out of me." He winced as he jerked his shirt open, sending buttons flying around the room. "Think I cracked a rib too."

Bree stared at his chest. "You were wearing a bulletproof vest?"

"Yep. It's a good thing too."

"But…your hand, it's—"

"Scraped it on a nail outside, climbing the fence from Mrs. Riley's house. Your dang gate was locked."

"Mrs. Riley?"

"Your neighbor. She gave me a spare key to your house. Came in the back door."

"Then…you're okay?"

"Did you not hear the part about cracked ribs?"

Ryland gently turned her to look at him. "Trent's like a cat. He's got about three or four more lives left in him."

"Gee, thanks for the concern, buddy."

Ryland ignored him and gently touched the side of her head.

She winced and ducked away. "Ouch."

"I thought you said you were okay."

"I am. He hit me with his gun. But I'm fine. What happened right before Kline tried to shoot you? Did Mrs. Kline hang up on him? Is that why he was enraged?"

"She was never on the phone. I called her before I came in, begged her to help, but she refused to talk to him. That was Faith on the screen."

She blinked. "You bluffed?"

"I bluffed." He grinned. "And it worked. You're alive. That's all that matters."

"You could have been killed!"

He scooped her up in his arms. The sound of sirens in the distance had him rolling his eyes. "I told them to come in silent, no sirens."

"Told you they'd manage to screw it up," Trent called out.

"You were right. For once. Come on, Bree. Let's get you to a hospital. You might have a concussion."

"What about my cracked ribs?" Trent called out.

"I'm sure Peterson will be happy to give you a ride when he gets here." He pressed a whisper-soft kiss against her lips. "We have to stop meeting like this. It's a hell of a way to start a relationship."

She blinked, then grinned. "It certainly is. Maybe you can tell me another way to start one on the way to the hospital."

"I'd rather show you." He winked, then carried her out the door.

Chapter Twenty-Five

"It's been a month since *The Incident*," Bree said, which was what she'd taken to calling that horrible day at her house with Kline holding a gun to her head. "I can't believe Peterson still won't let me come back to work. He's punishing me for not following all his silly rules." She frowned up at the darkening sky through the windshield of Ryland's Rover. It looked like they were going to finally get some snow.

"He's not punishing you." Ryland steered around a truck hauling a trailer of horses. "He couldn't let you go back until you were medically cleared after that nasty blow to your head."

"I had a mild concussion and a few stitches. No big deal. My doctor gave me a note to return to work two weeks later. That was two weeks ago."

"Has the therapist given you a note too?"

She crossed her arms. "I'm thinking about

seeing a different therapist. This one doesn't seem to like me."

Ryland chuckled. "Poor Bree. Those doctors can be so mean."

"They totally are!"

He laughed again, then slowed and turned left down a road she'd never noticed on their other trips. "At least with all that time off, you've been able to see a lot more of me."

She smiled. "True. Definitely a perk." She looked around. "Um, this isn't the way to Gatlinburg. Where are you taking us? We have another hour to go, and we won't make it to Prescott Mountain before dark if we don't hurry. I know you hate driving in the mountains at night."

"You think you know me that well, huh?"

"I do." She took his right hand in her left one. "It's been amazing spending these past few weeks with you. That's the only good part about Peterson refusing to let me return to work."

He squeezed her hand, then let go so he could use both hands on the wheel. This road was a lot bumpier than the main highway they'd been on.

"Is this a short cut?" she asked.

"Sort of." He could feel her questioning stare, but luckily, before she could ask any more questions, they reached the driveway. He slowed and turned the Rover up the long drive, glancing at her to gauge her reaction.

Her eyes widened as the beautiful vista opened up before them. He loved seeing the wonder and awe in her expression as she took in the acres of rolling hills, the thick trees that lined the massive property, the pretty little pond out front.

"Ryland, who lives here? It's incredible." Her eyes widened. "Oh my. Look at that house."

He grinned. Just as he'd hoped, she seemed just as blown away at the beauty of the two-story log cabin's honey-toned walls as he was the first time he'd seen it. He pulled to a stop in front and cut the engine.

"Daylight's a-wasting," he said. "Let's go."

"Go where?"

He hopped out of the Rover and strode to her side as she got out. "Come on. The owner gave me a key."

"A key. Why would the owner give you a key?"

"Do you ever stop asking questions?" he teased as he unlocked the front door.

"I'm a detective. It's my life's work to ask questions. But usually I'm much better at getting answers. What's going…" She stumbled to a halt just inside the two-story foyer, her gaze locked on the painting on the wall beside the knotty pine staircase. She pressed a hand to her chest, just over her heart, her eyes filling with tears. "Is that...is that my painting? The one I gave to Melanie?"

"I'm told it's an original, that there weren't any copies made."

She turned to face him, her eyes bright and misty. "Do I have to beg you to tell me what's going on? Because I'm about ready to."

He took both of her hands in his and pressed a soft kiss against her cheek. "I know that painting was sentimental to you, because it was originally your gift to your mom. I hated that you traded it to your friend to get information on the case. So I bought it back. That's the errand I had to run the day of The Incident."

"Oh, Ryland. You didn't have to do that. But thank you. That's so sweet. But why is it here? Why are we here?"

"Don't you know, Detective? Haven't you figured it out? I adore you, Bree. I love everything about you. I've never met someone who enjoyed their work the way I do, who craves the answer to every question, who refuses to give up until they follow every lead, pull every thread to see what unravels. You make me laugh at your crazy theories and leaps in logic. And then you humble me by being right most of the time. You've taught me there's more than one way to solve a case, that I should be flexible and more open to new ideas. I'm the better for having met you. And yet, the very thing that I love about you, your love for your work, is the one thing keeping us apart."

She blinked back tears and bowed her head. "You love your job too. You're talking about the commute, right? Two hours one way. You're worried that once I go back to my job, trying to maintain a long-distance relationship won't work. Is that it? You've rented this cabin for the weekend so we can have one last good memory together? And hung that painting, trying to make it special? Honestly, if that's the plan, to have one last glorious weekend together before we break up, then I'd rather you just take me home right now."

He gently tilted up her chin. "Bree, sweetheart, I didn't rent this cabin for a weekend fling. I bought it. For us. I don't want two days with you. I want forever. If that means splitting the difference between our two workplaces and moving here, then that's what I'll do. This place is almost the exact halfway point. I'm hopeful that you can handle a one-hour one-way commute to work from here. But if you don't want to move, then I'll deal with it. I'll travel an hour to work every day, an hour back. Then another hour to your place in Madisonville if that's the only way I get to see you."

Tears streamed down her face. "You would do that for me?"

"I'd do that and more. It may seem crazy after only knowing you for such a short time, but my heart knew you the first moment I saw you. You're everything to me, Bree. I love you. I'd be deeply honored if you'd agree to move in with me, and give the new commute a chance. But like I said, if you don't want to, it's okay. I'll do the driving for both of us."

For once, she seemed at a loss for words. He gently wiped the tears from her cheeks. "Bree, what's going on in that beautiful mind of yours?"

She sniffed, and drew a shaky breath. "I'm thinking that for a detective, you don't have a clue. I've been working with a real estate agent for the past two weeks trying to find someplace near the halfway point between both of our workplaces. But I don't have the budget you have, so I haven't had any luck." She laughed, smiling even as more tears streamed down her face.

He grinned. "Then you're okay with the plan? You'll give it a try?"

She nodded vigorously. "More than okay. You silly man. How could you ever think I'd say no? The Slayer case may have been your dream case. But you're my dream man. I half fell in love with you the moment you pulled me over the guardrail, saving my life. I fell the rest of the way when I found out you'd done that in spite of your fear of heights—a fear you've yet to explain to me but hopefully will at some point. It doesn't matter. Whatever is behind it, the fear is real. And you risked everything to rescue me. You're my hero, Ryland. You'll always be my hero."

His hands were shaking as he pulled her to him and ravaged her mouth with his. They kissed and kissed, the way she'd longed to for so very long. There was nothing in their way now, nothing keeping them apart. They loved each other. All this time she'd wondered if he did, and now she knew. And it was the most wondrous feeling ever. It gave her strength, made her feel whole and happier than she'd ever been. And it gave her hope for the future, one unshadowed by the past. All because of this amazing, gorgeous man who, by some miracle, seemed to love and cherish her the same way she loved and cherished him.

When he finally pulled back, he pressed one last soft kiss against her brow. His gaze searched hers, and then, slowly, he lowered one knee to the floor.

She stared at him, her mouth falling open as he pulled a black velvet box from his pocket and opened it to reveal the most beautiful diamond ring she'd ever seen.

"Yes," she said, holding out her hand.

"I haven't asked yet," he said, laughing.

"I'm a detective. I already knew the question."

He was still laughing as he slid the ring on her finger. "Just so there aren't any misunderstandings, when you move in here, you'll be moving in as Mrs. Beck. Is that your understanding as well?"

"Mrs. Clark-Beck, maybe?" She wrinkled her nose. "That doesn't flow very well, does it?"

"As long as I can call you my wife, I don't care what your last name is."

"Now that's a name I can live with."

He laughed and scooped her up in his arms. "Welcome home, my bride-to-be. Welcome home."

* * * * *

Look for more books in award-winning author Lena Diaz's miniseries, A Tennessee Cold Case Story, coming soon.

And if you missed the first book in the series, you'll find Murder on Prescott Mountain *wherever Harlequin Intrigue books are sold!*

Get 4 FREE REWARDS!

We'll send you 2 FREE Books plus 2 FREE Mystery Gifts.

Harlequin Romantic Suspense books are heart-racing page-turners with unexpected plot twists and irresistible chemistry that will keep you guessing to the very end.

FREE
Value Over
$20

YES! Please send me 2 FREE Harlequin Romantic Suspense novels and my 2 FREE gifts (gifts are worth about $10 retail). After receiving them, if I don't wish to receive any more books, I can return the shipping statement marked "cancel." If I don't cancel, I will receive 4 brand-new novels every month and be billed just $4.99 per book in the U.S. or $5.74 per book in Canada. That's a savings of at least 13% off the cover price! It's quite a bargain! Shipping and handling is just 50¢ per book in the U.S. and $1.25 per book in Canada.* I understand that accepting the 2 free books and gifts places me under no obligation to buy anything. I can always return a shipment and cancel at any time. The free books and gifts are mine to keep no matter what I decide.

240/340 HDN GNMZ

Name (please print)		

Address		Apt. #

City	State/Province	Zip/Postal Code

Email: Please check this box ☐ if you would like to receive newsletters and promotional emails from Harlequin Enterprises ULC and its affiliates. You can unsubscribe anytime.

Mail to the **Harlequin Reader Service:**
IN U.S.A.: P.O. Box 1341, Buffalo, NY 14240-8531
IN CANADA: P.O. Box 603, Fort Erie, Ontario L2A 5X3

Want to try 2 free books from another series! Call 1-800-873-8635 or visit www.ReaderService.com.